To j♡

Here's to dreams
coming true!

THE RESURRECTION OF BAYOU SAVAGE

Keep on pushin'!

Dean

Russell

THE RESURRECTION OF BAYOU SAVAGE

❀

Guitar Ghost Fighter

Robert "Dean" D Russell

iUniverse, Inc.
New York Lincoln Shanghai

The Resurrection of Bayou Savage
Guitar Ghost Fighter

iUniverse, Inc.

For information address:
iUniverse, Inc.
2021 Pine Lake Road, Suite 100
Lincoln, NE 68512
www.iuniverse.com

ISBN: 0-595-29599-1

CHAPTER 1

❀

Steve laughed. The whole purpose of his life for the last twenty years had been to resurrect the 200-year-old quantum corpse of Bayou Savage, Guitar Ghost-Fighter. That dream was flushed away by one memo from his boss, Director Oswalt. He should have seen it coming.

Bureaucracy had just now not only bruised, but also crushed Steve's twenty-year quest and his department dreams. He had given and lost over a thousand weeks of his life on this project. It seemed from the books Steve had read about Bayou Savage's life, since before his death in 2006, that politics played a part in his life, too, just as they did in Steve's now.

During a phone conversation discussing the memo, Steve recalled Oswalt mentioning, "To be honest with you, you never learned the political game; you never learned to schmooze the board. I tried to help, and I will continue to help you. I'll be over later tonight. You'll be working tonight, won't you?"

"Yes," Steve mumbled, shaking his head of brown hair, mixed with ever-more gray hair, and hung up the phone. Steve realized that the ongoing two-hundred-year experiment to revive or alter the suspended body of Bayou Savage was nearing an end.

In his quest to bring Bayou Savage back, Steve Johnson—commonly known as Hanger 19 Director—had practiced every technique and methodology available. Perseverance was the key, but the funding cut meant that Steve would be denied resources for unlocking the secret. His evolution of sensibility and hard work had just been demolished. He quietly reflected on how to tell Jed and the rest of the scientists. Most of them had been with him during his twenty-year directorship.

Steve attributed his tenure as a simple reflection of his hard work and his grasp of the quantum nature of the universe. He'd have to inform his team of scientists that they were all out of work. Where was the severed rabbit's foot when you needed it?

Steve knew that it would kill him, psychologically, to unhook the quantum interference field devices attached to the coffin. He looked around slowly and thought about the many decisions he had to make. Resting his arms on his old, worn oak desk, he pondered how the desk and all the relics of the quest had held up under the past twenty years of nicks and poundings. He hoped he looked better than they did. Right now, he sure didn't feel any better.

Steve vaguely remembered being preoccupied with some detail about mathematical space before the memo had wrecked his day. Wrecked his life. He was so close to bringing the body back from the dead. The secret was finally within reach. He had to make the choice to either accelerate the final experiment or start shutting down.

Blood rushed through his body and flushed his face. This was it. His decision was made. Steve looked down with custodial curiosity at the silver coffin in front of him. As he looked at it, he thought about the obstacles he would have to overcome if he were to go ahead tonight. But tomorrow night would probably be too late. Steve had made some enemies, and he knew that they wouldn't wait longer than a day to pounce on his departmental demise.

Here, deep in his secret lair—the Hangar 19 lab—was the mystery the Institute had kept quiet for over two centuries. His single purpose for the last two decades had been to bring Bayou Savage, Guitar Ghost Fighter, back to life. Of course there were no ghosts to fight, and there hadn't been since before Steve was born.

Hangar 19 had been named after the UFO folklore of the twentieth century. The urban legend was told of how the old Hangar 18 housed alien bodies for preservation and examination. On the surface, Hangar 19 looked like a regular hangar. According to all the rumors, however, it housed a regular ménage of results from thousands of supernatural investigations. That particular rumor was true, but only those with clearance knew the truth or had access to the facility.

The entrance was a security fanatic's dream, full of bizarre banalities designed to irritate anyone trying to get in to investigate. Every conceivable form of modern security had been installed for all visitors entering or leaving the hangar. The security system included wireless technology that transmitted camera images and conversations occurring at the entrance to the facility and then transmitted to the security control room. There was the biometric technology that was used at ATM machines all over the neofederation, implemented a bit differently at Hangar 19, including voice printing and signature verification.

Because of even internal security complexities, Hangar 19 had PIR's with an on-board database containing the digitized equivalents of actual and anticipated patterns of human movement. Whenever changes in infrared energy were detected, the pattern was digitized and compared to those in the database. Patterns matching human movement caused the unit to trip. Other patterns, although detected, were rejected, which substantially reduced false alarms.

The main floor was divided into three areas and housed thousands of artifacts, like a library, with rows of shelves labeled in alphabetical order. It was an orderly collection, divided into sections. One section was for devices used to fake supernatural events. Another displayed authentic devices used to produce psychic phenomenon. The last area housed the library of folklore, along with the conclusions from each investigation—mostly hard copy—with one small area dedicated to the Internet searches. There was one 10'x10' area, the lunar section, where events occurring during the full moon were kept, and one row discussed werewolf transformation and the influence of the lunar cycle.

Nowhere on the floor was there mention of a basement section. Everyone who worked at the Institute believed that something unusual was located beneath the main floor. The secret entrance was more than just a legend. The real entrance was located at the fringe of a parking garage. The personnel who worked in the basement did park in the basement level, but they had to go through a different undisclosed entrance first, which opened into a quarter-mile tunnel that led to the real entrance of the basement hangar.

The basement was divided into three areas: the laboratory, the testing rooms, and the crypt. Steve had tried for two decades to shut down the hemorrhage of gossip about the hangar. The rumors were understandable. In the absence of facts, people perceived their own paranoia as a foundation for pent-up imaginations. He smiled and thought to himself, "Part of the job, man; it's all part of the job." As he had been told in countless performance reviews, all in all, it was *his* job to control the gossip about this place. Unlike the original hangar, this hangar actually housed a body—and an artifact—that was the fabric of legends.

The artifact, a 1953 Fender Esquire guitar with unusual red pickups—called The Bloodstone Pickups—had remained here in the basement, the crypt, since 2006, along with the body. The guitar and body slept as one, almost as if they were entwined at death. They had both been picked over by a handful of cryogenic specialists, and a variety of other scientists who had visited the crypt. All of these highly educated, trained and sophisticated technicians had tried to revive the inert body of Bayou Savage, with a cure for whatever had killed or suspended him, unsuccessfully.

As Steve reflected, Brown, the Institute's CFO, walked into the room. He had that smug checkmate look on his face, and Steve was his target. He opened his mouth and said, "Steve, Steve, Steve! Sorry to hear that they're shutting you down." He smiled cynically as he continued. "The realities of this department were unusual and a waste of time and Institute money. The body you have wasted resources on has registered no temperature of any kind, and has confounded every scientist in charge of this stupid project. Steve, it's time to put all of your pet theories and solutions, and rumors you spread about me to bed." Steve knew Brown was enjoying this patronization, and it gnawed on him like vultures on a carcass under a blazing desert sun.

Brown walked over and stood nose-to-nose with Steve. Brown's larger nose was nearly pressing into the tip of Steve's smaller, aristocratic-like nose, almost like the barrel of a gun. Then Brown suddenly morphed a Cheshire grin. "No one has been able to solve the mystery. No one, no way, no how. You've learned to admit nothing, deny everything, and make accusations when someone has tried to blame you for failure. You have produced no tangible evidence. This place has been nothing but a rumor mill and specter—a damn phantom for late-night conversations and a real waste of resources."

Brown couldn't stop; he wanted to bury Steve with his anger, cynicism and ball-busting abuse. "Usually Steve, your rumors amuse me. I didn't mind the noise involving ghosts, space aliens, crop circles, and fallen angels.

But this talk of hidden bank accounts and my involvement was truly revolutionary. I consider this last bit of babble a futile exercise and a personal affront, so I got your department closed. You should have stayed with the entertaining rumors. Ah, I will miss the pinhead battles over your departmental resources and lack of planning."

Steve glanced at the cylindrical-shaped coffin and frowned to himself, saying nothing. Smiling, thinking about all the rumors he had created, it was humorous, certainly. The top of the coffin was clear and bulletproof. He looked more closely and saw a body frozen in time, existing in suspended animation without the traditional cryo-techniques. No numbing cold, no wires, and no tubes—nothing. A pristine tribute to research and what The Institute once was.

The Institute had somehow managed to put the body in this silver enclosure to protect Bayou Savage. No one had ever duplicated that feat. Brown walked over and stared down at the body, too.

"Don't worry, your sweetheart will be fine. He's not going anywhere, or at least he hasn't in the last 200 years. Don't you agree?" Brown laughed voraciously, like a lion ready for a kill.

It was two hundred and six years ago, to be exact. The decree, issued by an ancient Director named Quirk, was simple: *Keep the body in sight and protected.* Quirk's records had been distorted during the electronic record destruction of the war in 2012, and rumor was that he died mysteriously sometime before 2012. Director Oswalt had privately spoken of his belief that if ghosts ever resurfaced, like King Arthur, the body would return when humanity needed it the most.

Hangar 19 had housed the coffin this entire time, with research upon research project failing to produce any results. Then, one hundred years ago, with the advent of accessing memory with the prototype DNA enhancer, a new directive had been issued. Steve's predecessors had tried to acquire a tissue sample from the body to reactivate its memory. The scientists had no success, despite their many attempts. Now, for the past twenty-odd years, Steve had been the last in the long line of failures. Despite all the progress in DNA memory refinement, Steve was no closer than any of the others had been.

All the experts he hired confirmed that if a tissue sample could be procured, the memory could be reactivated. If they had the mechanism to determine what had kept the body in its current quantum state, they could domesticate the electrons—something they'd been trying to do for years. Everyone felt sorry for Steve: those who were aware of his true work and those who didn't have clue. They read his body language, and it didn't speak of a person who had triumphed over adversity. It screamed out in pain and anguish with every step, "I have worked my ass off and have nothing to show for it."

The encased body was an enigma, like the Shroud of Turin, but this body had the aura of tragedy because of Bayou's suicide. The Shroud of Turin was a centuries-old linen cloth that bore the image of a crucified man, presumably Jesus. No one knew if the Shroud of Turin was really the cloth that wrapped His crucified body, or simply a medieval forgery. The Shroud had been the single most studied artifact in human history, before the discovery of Bayou Savage.

To Steve, the suicide was immaterial. His problem was justifying the department's substantial budget and the lesser results. Jed Harris, one of the senior scientists, had asked at least a thousand times, "Steve, how could a body suspend itself in a virtual quantum state? Further, how could that body survive for over two hundred years with no change?"

The Great Religion War and the Neutron Bombs of 2012 had destroyed all the records available prior to that date. He had pried into every government secret stash he could find, with no results.

The Institute had tried to save the world from the 2012 cataclysm. They were a clandestine group to all the governments in the world. They pumped out many psychic rescues throughout the years. They predicted and shared information with all the world leaders in a marathon media blitz in 2111. The problem was that no one knew how the catastrophe would occur. Most thought it would be an asteroid or comet on a fatal collision course with Earth. No one expected the Religious War. No one expected the Neutron Bombs. No one expected anything to actually *happen*.

The Institute's prediction was based on the ancient Mayan calendar. The calendar had predicted that a civilization would mass destruct in 2012. The Great Religious War had been a population, culture, information, and virtual destroyer. The Neutron Bombs wiped out all electronic memories. The Mayan predictions had made believers out of those who survived.

Bombs and jihads had shattered the confidence of an arrogant world. Similar to the story about Noah in the primitive Old Testament, few had listened. The former USA was the only country that tried to react in a quasi-proactive way. The Institute's warnings were ignored. Civilization was plunged into near total destruction. The Mayans must have had one hell of a psychic; they foresaw the catastrophe and had been the first to give the exact year.

The world was now a collection of savage empires competing against each other. Civilization went through enormous changes after the wars. It became a chess player's dream. Nations did away with civility. Spiritual complacency was replaced by spiritual terror. The process of dying was now an ugly, worldwide, unvarnished reality.

The Institute, determined to survive, had endured by seeking out metaphysical prediction. Crystals, tarot cards, any and all types of metaphysical components helped the Institute to be prepared. The USA annexed Canada, Central and South America, and they became a neofederation. The USA remained the strongest economy in the world, but the population—of the USA alone—had dropped from 300 million to 85 million by 2013. The world population had dropped from 8 billion to 3 billion. The Institute recruited the best scientists and purchased the best resources available in that time period. Hav-

ing worked on cloning the DNA of great psychics, with little success, they realized that the technology wasn't advanced enough to create a clone with the
same psychic powers of any of the dead great masters. Since the death of the
body in front of Steve, all psychic power had essentially ceased.

Steve, and many other scientists before him, believed that the silver coffin
and its occupant were some sort of atonement for progress. A multitude of
every type of scientist, conducting every probe in the neoscience arsenal, using
every conceivable trick up their educated sleeves, had tried to unlock the secret
of the body. No one had had any luck. They just couldn't figure it out.

It didn't help that Steve was considered one of the best quantum scientists
left in the world. He had graduated at the top of his class and had broken
ground in quantum electromechanical engineering research, studying the
principles of decoherence and its degrees of freedom. Despite his many accom-
plishments, Steve felt that he had become the laughingstock of the scientific
community.

Plus, Brown had spread many rumors about his department's lack of
progress, and Steve had become Brown's favorite whipping boy.

Steve had initially taken the Institute job feeling supremely confident that
he would triumph over the fabled enigma. He had told the Board that he
would—in less than a year—isolate and accomplish active memory viewing of
whatever lay in the coffin. Steve concluded that the body was evidence of quan-
tumness interference effects that had vanished from the classical world. The
body looked like a gold flickering holograph. The technical term was "quantum superposition," which meant the body was shooting back and forth
between different dimensions. He had confidently informed the board that the
decoherence of this mystery was the interaction between the quantum system
and a complex environment.

After measuring the body, the environment must have held some kind of
indelible record of the quantum event. The record could be carried off into
space on the backs of photons, or could be dissipated among a billion particles
within the quantum system itself. He would merely track the interference pattern and unlock the cause.

That pipe dream was twenty years ago. Steve often regretted that brash,
overconfident remark about him solving the puzzle within such a short time.
Three hundred and sixty-five days wasn't really that long a time, after all. It had
come back to haunt him many times. Twenty years of hard work, and he was
finally closing in on success. He could feel the breath from the kiss of his
dream. Now he figured he had about ten hours to try and succeed.

Jed asked, "What was that about?" after Brown was gone. Steve didn't answer. Jed started talking about the experiment they had planned to conduct next month, called *The Big One*. "The problem is the body is compounded by the lack of entropy. Newton said for every action there is a reaction, and I think it's time to kick some quantum ass." Steve softly declared.

The dilemma surfaced again. Steve's hazel eyes were looking at a scientific conundrum—the only true supernatural event existing in the world. Cold chills covered the length of his arm as he pensively touched the coffin. Somehow, by constantly touching the coffin, Steve felt closer to a solution. Steve recognized that some of his colleagues believed that it was a genuine supernatural miracle and that nothing could access the body except divine force.

The Cryo-Institute scientists wanted the physiological insight to the body's homeostasis. The mystery had to be solved. Steve's egomania had been eliminated, humbled, and reduced, down to this last demon of a quest. This single-mindedness left him lonely; he had no girlfriend, never married, didn't have children, and no friends. He spent all of his time trying to crack an undecipherable code. He was the typical serious intellect, one who was weak with social applications. He could tell you what was wrong with your life, but he wasn't able to fix his own. However, Steve was more bold and audacious than many of his predecessors. He was also abrupt and said what was on his mind. His staff seemed to appreciate his focus and intensity. With exacting care, Steve opened the coffin. The only light in the basement room was focused on Bayou Savage's detailed and mysterious face. The face was roughly forty years of age. A portrait of humor and heartbreak painted the features in the coffin. Lots of smile lines—yet sadness—permeated the frozen mask, giving it a haunted look. Steve's last assistant had called the coffin's occupant "frostfish." This was because no recovery could be made of any body temperature. The prevailing theory was that the body was in a quantum state. The body was free-floating in the dimensional sea. The multidimensional hyperspace of quantum physics was the only explanation. In lay terms, the body in the coffin was surfing through multiple dimensions. It appeared to be in one place, yet it wasn't. For twenty years, Steve had explained it to new employees, with a chuckle "It's easy to explain something that is basically unexplainable."

CHAPTER 2

❈

Jade toiled through the labyrinth of the Institute's History Department for help in learning what had formed the facial features on the face in the coffin. Jade Grimm was a Doctorate Historian at the Institute. As the head historian and resident expert on all things related to Bayou Savage, she had been a godsend to Steve. Jade had entangled him in the history of the person in the coffin. She had the ability to look at supernatural events in history from a clinical, scientific view. Jade was known as one of the brightest historians to have graced the Institute's halls, and her reputation was truly deserved.

Steve had been Jade's "good-time boy." She dated him, got tired of his dogmatic tenacity to break the mystery in the coffin, and broke off the relationship for someone more interested in her. The problem was that Jade was almost as dedicated to the experiment as Steve, and she usually ended up being dumped in her other relationships for the same reasons she had wanted to be rid of Steve.

Steve had met Jade at a bar near the Institute. He noticed her luscious red lips, thick red hair and wide-set brown eyes, swaggered up to her and asked, hazel eyes twinkling, "Would you like a gin and platonic, or do you prefer scotch and sofa?"

Most of the Institute people were eggheads. Steve offered boldness and humor, qualities that Jade was starved for. When they hooked up again, after the first breakup, Steve said, "Levi Strauss should pay you royalties for wearing those pants!"

He was clever, at least, she thought to herself. With Steve, it was a genuine compliment; he had a gentle touch and knew how to move a woman. Jade's looks and brains were both first-class, but she was a humble woman Jade's secret weapons were her photographic memory and attention to detail. She also had the uncanny ability to convey any emotion by using her eyes. Over the past few years, Jade had directed large sums of time and money into the Bayou Savage research project. All data concluded that the body was "Bayou Savage, son of Razor Savage."

The news of Steve's department closing down finally got to Jade. She felt sick and knew that the rumor was probably true.

They had tried to clear away the legend and execute true historical research to explain the humorous, yet sad, look on the face in the coffin. Ten years earlier, Steve and Jade had attempted to get a sample of DNA from the body for the clone experiment. It had been a dismal failure and had destroyed half the lab. Steve had to explain to Brown and the Board what had gone wrong. How do you tell funders that Steve and his scientists had been technologically premature and had focused on the *body's* physics, not the guitar? The experiment was a catastrophic accident. The quantum-measuring device caused instantaneous collapse of the wave function and destroyed a good portion of the lab and critically hurt three scientists.

After his experiment, Bayou Savage's epistemology and risk were in alignment. Steve thought he had figured out the interference pattern and believed he could tap into the field that was guarding the real body. During the process, Jed learned that the body was in many worlds simultaneously, and the expense of trying to bring the body back, using the famous inverse quantum Zeno effect, backfired.

Steve blew up half the lab again, but he learned how powerful the mystic self-replicator force was that held the static body. The secret was somehow related to the guitar. Now, ten years later—twenty all told—he was ready to try again. He fingered the memo in his pocket and felt an extreme pang of fear mixed with paranoia course through him. "Damn," he thought, "it's just not fair."

Steve had written a white paper for the Institute scientists, indicating that the body was a singularity and its existence was an illusion in this plane. Debates over whether the body was breathing, not breathing, alive or frozen, were hard to prove, since no measurements were possible. The illusion of the body unfolded in a macro-continuous, nonlinear fashion, but in reality the body was discontinuous and linear in this plane.

Steve believed that the state of the body was prevalent upon the artifact: the guitar. The one thing that every other predecessor had thought dead and immaterial was the one hope of breaking through the stasis. The yellow guitar had burnt fried edges with reddish Bloodstone pickups that somehow looked alive. Jed had told him that there seemed to be a magic presence surrounding the Fender. The guitar was invulnerable, and as far as Steve knew, immortal. The guitar envisioned and reverberated like the legendary Excalibur. It still had all six strings attached to the scorched machine heads. If the experiment could reactivate the guitar, they would have to replace those machine heads. According to legend, they had melted during an epic ghost battle that Bayou Savage barely survived.

Jade's historians knew the legend of the guitar. It was the famous ghost-fighting, twenty-first-century Fender guitar. Jade was never sure if the guitar fought ghosts, or was used in fighting ghosts. Guitar history was something she did know about. She said that this was a guitar professionals used and younger musicians begged their parents to spring for. It was expensive and invaluable to those who bought a good Fender. The historians were perplexed and amazed concerning the strange markings on the neck and the unusual color of the pickups. From what they could discover, no one in that time period had made red pickups.

Jade believed the guitar was interfering with the internal quantum measurements. She believed that the guitar—and only the guitar—was responsible for the quantum coherence after watching Steve's last experiment. Steve's next experiment was to break the quantum coherence of the guitar, but obviously this wouldn't happen, since he was going to be an Institute ghost within 300 hours. This would cause the body to suffer an irreversible loss of quantum measurement, which might cause death. But up Steve's sleeve was a new twist that involved capturing a low-entropy state to get the result the Institute wanted. If he were successful, the body would sustain itself beyond detonation.

Jade smiled down at the disc she was holding, able to see her own reflection. When she shared this with Steve, he was just not going to believe it! This was the biggest moment of her historical career, and Steve was going to be very, very surprised. She had planned to wait until next month, but with the rumors floating around, she knew the time was now. She smiled again as she went to contact him.

Steve believed that if nothing interfered with the body, there was no evolutionary timescale that could comprehend the longevity of its existence—not on any measurement scale that he knew of. Jade had just called and received new insight into that timeline preceding Bayou's death that Steve didn't know about. This information might impact his last experiment. She had started to cry and said she would call back later. He wanted to cry with her.

CHAPTER 3

❀

As Steve looked into the coffin, the empty hollow face with closed eyes met his gaze. If he didn't move the experiment up to tonight, if he didn't succeed tonight, it might be centuries before anyone else would try. The frozen face would remain the same for hundreds of years unless some outside stimulus saved the project.

He hit the button that signaled an emergency department meeting. Time to let everyone know the new mandate and let the employees know their options. He figured those options to be: die in the effort, a distinct possibility; or get fired for squandering department resources when they knew they were being shut down; the last option was the dream—to finally succeed in their twenty-year quest, but there were no guarantees that they could do it.

Steve looked at the group and took a deep breath before he spoke. He couldn't make eye contact, because they were a team, but his body language told the scientists more than Steve realized. "I received a memo this morning. We have 30 days to shut the department down. Some of you will probably be reassigned, but I don't have details yet. The rest of you will probably have to sign a non-disclosure agreement and get a severance package." For a few seconds there was stunned silence.

The extraverts surfaced first, making angry noises, while the introverts looked down at the floor as they processed the change. A few grumbled and said they had already heard some rumors. The consensus was that Brown, that asshole, had finally found a way to shut them down. Brown was probably laughing with the Board members right now, because the Institute might actually make the shareholders money, for once, instead of losing money consistently on the Bayou Savage project. Steve could see Brown swirling some single malt scotch in a nice heavy low-ball glass, telling the Board, "You'll never believe it, but I've found a way to make the Institute money and put that cocky Steve Johnson on his way out within 24 hours! Of course we'll pay him for 30 days, but he's packing his shit up right now," Brown would laugh boisterously and clink the iced tumblers with the other Board members.

Steve turned his thoughts to his own team of scientists. "I'm proud of all of you!" Steve proclaimed. The world of psychic science had been dead for over 200 years. There had not been a single verified instance of real psychic phenomenon during that period of time, except with this quantum body and artifact.

Steve paused, and then said, "Damn I'm proud that we had the chance to work on a true intertwinement of a psychic and quantum occurrence." He hesitated and thought of how he was going to handle the hardest part of this little speech.

"Today is the last time this project will be worked on, but all of you will be paid until the end of the month." When the questions starting flying, Steve held up his hand warding them off and felt the headache from earlier come roaring back. He listened and waited as the shockwave washed over them. Now was the critical part. He wondered who would say it first.

His best scientist, Jed, cleared his throat and spoke the words that Steve had been waiting to hear. Jed yelled, "Quiet, everyone calm down!"

He looked up at Steve, "I estimate we have tonight to pull this off. Brown and his vultures will have this place picked clean by tomorrow. I say let's go ahead tonight; screw getting reassigned or fired. I spent 20 damn years on this, and I refuse to just quit and walk away."

Steve looked around and spoke. "My Level IV clearance, education, and Brown experience deem you are right. It will all be wasted anywhere else but in this room. I have always recruited the best, and I gave you the freedom to explore options for obtaining a sample of Bayou. All of our particular quantum specialties have led to what will now be our last experiment. We know the guitar is a conduit. All we need is to create a nanosecond of time so that the feed of quantum information correlates back to this dimension."

The scientists looked at each other. Jed looked around and spoke, getting a nod from Steve. They both knew that Jed was the unofficial team leader, and the proposal to take the ultimate risk tonight had to come from one of them. Steve was glad it was Jed who had taken the lead.

Jed asked for a show of hands on who wanted to stay tonight. Everyone raised their hands, even old Al, the senior scientist in the room.

Steve looked around with a sense of pride. Without melodrama, he said, "Tonight, either we bring Bayou Savage's memories back to life or we blow the whole damn lab up again. This time it's all or nothing."

He continued. "Think hard people; don't join unless you want to. If you don't want to, it's ok, the Institute and I have enjoyed working with you. You were all a true pleasure to work with. You also all know the risk involved.

"I'm asking, if you choose not to participate, that you give the rest of us until tomorrow. Either way, I'm going ahead. For those of you who are staying, let's get going."

Just as the meeting broke up, the phone rang. Each scientist was getting ready for the last experiment. Steve's reverie was broken as he picked up the phone and heard Jade's voice; his heart fluttered a bit as she talked about her latest discovery.

"Steve, as I told you I found some new data." Jade sounded excited. Steve could picture her as she was talking. He'd be seeing her a few hours from now, even though she didn't know it.

"We found a historical artifact of a first cousin's of Mist, Bayou Savage's daughter, on a buried computer drive email. The hard drive was jagged and fried, but we roughed out a few historical messages." She continued. "We managed to pull out an interesting excerpt. The dates and times are authentic, and it's as close as we have come to a firsthand report of Bayou's existence through his daughter's first cousin. The only other collaborative evidence is Director Quirk's account here at the Institute."

"Okay, Jade, tell me what you found. Better yet, come over now. Tonight is our last night as a functioning unit." Steve directed her, trying to keep his voice steady, trying not to get too excited about her news or show the anger he felt about Brown's perceived *coup de grace*.

She could hear the excitement rising in his voice. She laughed and said, "Steve, listen up. This is big! I know tonight is the last night. But if you do make contact with Bayou," she took a deep breath and continued, knowing that in a few hours in would all be over, one way or the other, "it will prove this is the first proof that the electronic signature from the Savage family is legitimate, and not a forged counterfeit."

"The email states that the cousin had an email from Mist. The information was relayed that her father was fighting ghosts with her grandfather. He fought these ghosts with a guitar that had special magical supernatural powers. She was worried that her father might get himself killed and that the cousin shouldn't be surprised if they lost their grandfather, because he was even crazier than her father." Jade paused to catch her breath.

"She also mentioned something else you might find interesting. Mist reported that Bayou had personal dynamics with someone named 'Leslie,' who also fought ghosts with something called the "Bloodstone!"

Steve felt his spirits rising. "The only recorded history until now had been Director Quirk's reports." This was news! Steve thought to himself.

Jade continued, "The email said that Mist was intrigued by her father's excitement, saying that Bloodstones are normally green with red overtures, but this Bloodstone was solid with reddish amber. She said that Bayou had a background as a lapidarian and had never heard of this."

The fine hairs on Steve's neck stood up straight. Only those in Steve's inner circle at the Institute were familiar with this particular data on the Bloodstone. Jade continued. "That was one of the first clues that this historical Bayou *find* was genuine. The counterfeiters out to make money assumed that the Bloodstone in the legends was a true-natured Bloodstone, which was green with red markings. Anyone who had studied geology or had lapidary training would have guessed a green stone with red markings."

The Bloodstone involved with the Bayou history had no green; that nugget of information had saved the Institute time and money. There had been many charlatans attempting to sell countless fake reproductions, but the Institute was wary of the Bloodstones that kept cropping up as being the "real" Bloodstone.

Jade paused and then continued. "Steve, the last thing the cousin wrote in her email was that Mist said her father was depressed after Razor died. That was the end of the captured conversation. That's it, my friend. I know it's confusing, but this is as close as we have ever come to verifying Bayou's existence."

Jade was a purist. She didn't accept data distortion or speculation. She had opinions, but you had to pry them out of her.

Steve considered the new information. He didn't care if Bayou *had* committed suicide. The carousel pursuit Steve had been on for so long didn't factor in the reason. Some reason had put this body in a state of quantum-suspended animation. Of course the bigwigs at the Institute would feel an integrity breakdown if their biggest champion of the psychic wars had killed himself. That information, if verified, would put a gothic-like fascination back into the legend.

When King Arthur was a young boy, he drew a sword called "Excalibur" from a stone. One version of the legend stated that the sword was made at Avalon from a sarsen stone from Avebury or Stonehenge. Whoever drew the sword from the stone was the true King of England, so Arthur was crowned. In AD 537, King Arthur was fatally wounded in a fight and was taken to Avalon, an island in a lake inhabited by sorceresses. That was where Arthur stayed suspended in time. That was the only recorded example of a body being suspended by a magic force that Steve had ever heard of.

Nothing in recorded history could accomplish the quantum suspension of Bayou Savage. The joke was that history contained two syllables: "his-story." The first four gospels in the New Testament were written at least thirty years—at a minimum—after the time of Jesus' death. Steve and Jade were drinking and discussing the Bible one night. She had informed Steve, "Mark was the oldest of the four gospels and was written circa AD 70. Matthew and Luke were written between AD 70 and 85 and John somewhere around AD 110."

Steve teased Jade on her end of the phone about her subtle ambivalence to subjectivism.

Steve asked, "Jade, what do you think about Bayou and the supposed suicide? You know more about Bayou than anyone alive." Steve knew what she was thinking before she responded to his question. She would have numerous misgivings. They both knew that she was the expert. She wanted hard data and also wanted separate collaborations of the same data.

Jade began, "This new information confirms an outside corroboration of Quirk's account. We have three finites. First, Razor, Mist, and Bayou actually lived. Second, there now is an outside recorded history of the guitar and the Bloodstone." She paused to take a breath. "Third, Bayou was depressed at the time of his death. Excuse me, at the time of his entrance to the quantum-suspended state."

Steve laughed. There had been way too many sitcoms, minifilms, documentaries, cults, and electronically hosted conversations on the legend of Bayou Savage. Different volunteers, excited about the *truth* behind the legend, had recruited their versions of the actual Bayou history. Of course there had been no prohibition against fictitious constructs.

"Jade, do you believe that Bayou somehow committed suicide using the guitar and Bloodstone?" Steve wanted her opinion, because it was objective. He never had to give a cease-and-desist order to stand down on the particulars of the legend with her. Jade was not into making a profit or a name for herself through her research; she was the truest historian Steve had ever met.

"Steve, what are you asking?"

"I'm asking what you think really happened to him. Not what did Director Quirk's archive relay and this email say. What do you personally think happened to him?"

Jade paused. "I think Bayou suffered from post-traumatic stress syndrome after his parents died. I believe this led to a failure of a rational emotive state, which in turn led to his demise. I believe that he didn't fight that last battle. He gave up. I think his initiative was destroyed and that the Institute, which now venerates him, let him down in his final days and gave him no emotional support. I further think he was a splendid example of what the world needs most in this time: a tragic hero. I think it explains his continual cult status and why it will continue."

The line was quiet as Steve digested Jade's words. This had been a significant discourse, and he didn't want the moment to end. She had just put it all together. She had presented a proud mental topographical musing. Was this information too late? Steve wondered. He thought of how to invite her over for the grand finale.

Jade had tied the psychological and historical facts together with her own identified cause and effects. Steve admitted to himself that he had missed the post-traumatic stress factor, but not her Institute perdition contribution. He was in agreement with her statements. Due to his unique position, Steve had talked with many Bayou experts throughout the years and wished for what he called the "Pinocchio effect." This effect would ensure that every time the experts strayed from reality, their noses would grow.

Jade told him, "The ancient Greeks had a concept they called *eating the taboo*. As a path to liberty, they would deliberately break any and all of their culture's prevailing taboos." The legend of Bayou had been eaten, digested, and regurgitated. Jade had stated that there had been some pretty elaborate rationalizations surrounding the Bayou legend, and that somewhere between them all was the truth.

His thoughts were interrupted by a video message from Brown. He didn't open it right away, and tried to finish thinking. He wished to be able to franchise Jade's opinion to the world, starting with the entire Institute and all of its subsidiaries. Bayou had lived and fought at the height of psychic warfare, and then disappeared. No one knew much about him, except that he had surfaced when he was about forty years old and disappeared three years later. No one in the outside world even knew what Bayou had looked like, other than the privileged few who had tried to decipher the secret.

The Institute, though, knew exactly what he looked like. What the Institute wanted to know was why all the psychic manifestations had disappeared at the same time Bayou disappeared. The Institute had an energy field with a body in it that could be seen, but not accessed; that quest had been his department's mission.

The only reliable histories gleaned were from quick field reports filed by Quirk, and he had died roughly at the same time as Bayou. After Quirk's death, history was quiet and no one seemed to care—until 2012.

Steve broke the silence, "Jade, can you come over tonight around 11:30-ish?"

"Why?" she queried. "Tonight is Halloween, and I might go Trick-or-Treating."

Steve laughed. "Well, I think we might have figured out how to access the DNA data for a memory scan and might possibly break the quantum state." The line was silent.

After a pregnant pause, she came back with a typical Jade comment. "I'm not authorized to actually see the body. Also, I thought you were waiting until next month. So, it's definite then—the news of Brown shutting you down, you have to do it tonight because there won't be a next month." That was it: no disappointment, no excitement, just a fact. If Steve accessed Bayou's memory, he needed someone who was objective. Not one of the cryptic Bayou cult followers who couldn't see the paradigm of what the actual Bayou was like or understand like a true historian who had studied the time period.

"Jade, I have your access! I know it's short notice, but can you be here tonight? We're already set up, and I have requested and received permission for you to attend tonight's affair. As a matter of fact, we were going to conduct the experiment next month, but Brown and his fellow crew have pronounced us dead in thirty days."

"Is there any luck we can pull from doing this on Halloween?"

"In 1517, Martin Luther took a stand on it. In 1926 Houdini made a final exit on it. In 1938 Orson Wells perpetrated a national hoax on it. Seventy percent of the United American Federation opens up their houses on it. Fifty percent more holographic images are created by parents taking pictures of their kids, and the Federation spends more than 65 billion dollars celebrating it. Due to the history of psychic events on All Soul's Day, tonight is perfect. The Celts of ancient Britain, Scotland, Ireland, and northern France marked the harvest end the return of herds from the pasture and the wisdom *the light that loses, the night that wins.*"

Jade continued, "More importantly, it was the festival of Samhain, also known as Halloween, ShadowFest, Martinmas, or Old Hallowmas. Since man has been alive, the Last Harvest is a time when the Earth nods a sad farewell to the God, who will once again be reborn of the Goddess, and the cycle continues. This is time for reflection, the time to honor the Ancients who have gone on before us, and the time of divination. As we contemplate the Wheel of the Year, we come to recognize our own part in the eternal cycle of Life. This means tonight could be the most important night that the last 20 years of research has led up to." Steve thought a moment, and then added, "If we try to reconstitute the memory of Bayou Savage, we might also find a spirit capable of revealing futures. The past has suggested that spirit contact on this night has revealed future marriages, windfalls, as well as illnesses and deaths.

"Our modern scholarship suggests Druidic origin and practices. Pomona, the Roman goddess of the harvest, had her festival celebrated on the first of November. So the window between October 31st and November 1st might be the most fortuitous time for us to break the quantum coma. The only thing we know about Bayou is that he came from a long line of religious men, basically preachers, and his whole family was from the Southern United States."

Steve laughed. "Well, Jade, if I die in this attempt, I might end up a tragic hero myself."

Jade laughed with him and said, "With an offer like that, Mr. Johnson, how could a historian refuse? I'll be there at 11 P.M. for set up. I assume that you have the holographic recorder—the video recorder, as you call it—in place? And by the way, what did the predictors give you as a chance for success?" Jade knew that he had the videos set up, and also that he must be confident of his chance for success.

"Yes, everything is getting ready. According to the team, we're looking at a 60% chance of success."

Steve thought for a moment and considered a scenario that brought a fierce stab of jealousy—and something else he couldn't identify. What if he brought Bayou back from the dead and Jade fell in love with him? His chest ached. The scholarly Steve Johnson had a weird premonition of the future, and knew it had to be a case of nerves. What else could it be?

CHAPTER 4

❀

At eleven, Jade walked through the door. The first thing she saw was Brown and Oswalt talking with Steve. Brown was in Steve's face, smiling. Oswalt stepped in between the two and Jade ran over to help, because from her angle it looked as if something ugly was about to happen.

Oswalt said, "I agree with Steve; his scientists want to do this last experiment, and I will sign an agreement that I'm giving my permission to conduct the experiment. They chose to turn down their severance pay." That stopped Brown dead in his tracks, and Jade thought she could see the little money signs flashing in his eyes.

Bastard Brown, only caring about himself, said, "If everyone signs a financial agreement which I will write up now, then I agree. Oswalt, you do know how much power this experiment will consume, don't you?"

Oswalt looked oppositionally at Brown. "Brown, as long as I'm in charge, I ultimately make the decisions. Steve, go ahead, screw the signed agreements. Let's see what happens first.

Brown, his face bright red and eyes flashing with anger, vengeance and jealousy, said, "Bullshit! Oswalt, I'm calling the board now. This is exactly what we were afraid would happen. That's why I'm here."

Oswalt stared at him, and spoke in low monotone tone, but his voice indicated that he wanted to throttle Brown. "If you contact anyone, I will let them know about you and your assistant. I have the hotel bills. I have recorded videos made by her husband. He is now putting the final touches on his alienation-of-affection lawsuit. I was trying to work this as an out-of-court settlement."

Now it was Brown's turn to stare. Everyone standing around stared at him, too. Most had heard the rumors about how Brown hired only the most attractive women. Admiring beautiful people is one thing, but having an affair on company time, which could result in a potentially pending lawsuit, was a different matter.

Brown smiled his Cheshire cat smile and turned to face Steve. "OK, Mr. Hotshot, take your best shot. It'll be rewarding to watch twenty years of wasted research and Institute money end tonight. Get on with your little experiment, just please make it fast. I have things to do." Brown ended speaking gruffly.

Steve smiled cynically back. "Yes, I guess you do. For starters, apologizing to your lover's husband would be good." Brown said nothing, turned his back and walked to his pre-assigned post.

Steve felt a flush of relief. He had been waiting for ages to put that bastard in his place, and it felt good. Now he had to get on with the experiment. Everyone in the lab was at his or her post. Jade turned and smiled when she looked at Steve. Most of these scientists had a common 10-year history during the great failed experiment. Jade noticed the Kevlar vests they were wearing and smiled. Old memories die—hard, especially when you blow up a perfectly good lab.

Everyone had grown to know and appreciate Jade. If there was a question about myths, legends, poetry, art, music, ritual worship, or even naughty historical behavior, she was the one to ask.

Jed asked Jade years ago—in his best scientific manner—how to meet women. He never forgot her response. "A smile goes a million miles; start there, then probe." Jed had asked on what topics to probe; again, without hesitation, Jade replied, "Current events, weather, common interests, pet passions, pet peeves; don't sound too faint or hesitant."

Persisting, Jed had asked for advice on his introductory first line. Jade hesitated briefly before she responded. Steve had just walked over and she wanted to answer Jed before Steve gave Jed some of his manly advice. She smiled at Jed, held out her hand, and said in a straightforward manner, "What a pleasure to meet you."

Jed never forgot that conversation; it had actually helped smooth his first meeting with his future wife. Before Jed proposed, he called Jade one last time for advice. She had suggested that he read a poem by the ocean before he proposed to his intended. Impress her with his romantic performance, and then surprise her with the ring. Jed, who never had quite figured out the value in this beat-around-the-bush approach, had asked pointblank what poem he

should read. Jade burst out laughing, knowing that Jed's fiancée would probably figure out he had help with this.

She had reached over and grabbed her favorite Wordsworth poem, "The
Prelude," Book Second, and started to read the old 19th century poet.

> I would walk alone, Under the quiet stars, and at that time, Have felt
> whate'er there is of power in sound, to breathe an elevated mood,
> by form, Or image unprofaned; and I would stand, If the night
> blackened with a coming storm, Beneath some rock, listening to
> notes that are, The ghostly language of the ancient earth, Or make
> their dim abode in distant winds, Thence did I drink the visionary
> power...

Jade put the book down and gave him a purely logical look. "You then pro-
claim that this visionary power has given you the gift to see both of your
futures, then give her the ring!" Jed thought the whole thing sounded bogus,
but it worked surprisingly well. His wife never asked Jed how he had come up
with the poem, but he suspected that she knew Jade had contributed. She knew
and liked Jade, as everyone else did. Jed never officially thanked Jade, but he
had invited her to come to their wedding, which was his way of saying thanks.

Steve looked over at the clock. It was getting close to *showtime*. One hour to
midnight and the contact. He looked down at the body again, surrounded by
the coils of installed object permanence field machinery. Even though they
couldn't make contact with the body, they had, during a nanosecond contact,
made connection with the charred remnant of the legendary guitar beside it.
The equipment was set up. The lasers, the functionality wave carriers, all had
set up resonance with the periphery of the pickup on the charred guitar. Steve
had given up on the body years ago, after the failed experiment. He realized
that the guitar was the transducer of the effect—to get to the memory he had
to integrate the atomic projectiles feeding the body.

If he could immobilize a sample of DNA, he could run the memory effect.
Steve worried that there might be other samples of DNA included in the sample, which would produce what was called the "polytheistic" effect. He wasn't
too worried, though; if he could access the memory, he would know the identity of the DNA holder. Even then, any memory he accessed would have
incredible historic value.

Through rigorous scientific research, using the Design of Experiments
(DOE), Steve learned that the body was protected by an energy source, which

was somehow transduced through the guitar. There was something about the guitar pickups that enveloped the body in suspended quantum animation.

Steve looked at the computer and quantum stabilizing units. He thought of whom he'd have to contact in his personal life in case something went wrong. He realized, with sudden clarity, that the answer was *no one*. All of his relatives were dead. Steve's precise brain insisted, before he conducted this experiment, that he tie up the loose ends in his life, but there were none; the only loose end was in this room with him.

Steve looked over and made eye contact with Brown. Brown shot him a *Why don't you just quit and walk away* look. Steve ignored him and made a mental note not to look at him again for the rest of the night. He watched Brown walk over to a pacing Oswalt. "Damn, shut this idiocy down. It's a waste. It's always been a waste. Damn you, Oswalt, we all know Steve is your little prodigy, but this time he's so far off the mark he wouldn't be able to get the eight ball in the hole in a million years!"

Jed walked up and said, "Look, this experiment has consumed the majority of my life. I know you don't give a shit, but for the rest of us, this is our life. If you can't sit there and be quiet, then leave!"

Brown looked to Oswalt for support. Oswalt looked straight into Brown's eyes. "Brown, sit down and shut up or leave. Don't you get it? I'm saying yes, and they can get on with their work without your constant annoyances."

Steve turned on the recording videos and once again went through the procedure, step-by-step, in his mind. If they had conducted the experiment next month like they had planned, he would have made sure Jed was located out of harm's way. He couldn't afford for anything to happen to him. Jed would have been his apparent heir. Jed, the kid with spunk and brains, was a solid, honest person who didn't take shortcuts. But that was over and he couldn't allow himself to be distracted by thinking about lost futures—not now.

He smiled at his own ego being the advocate of the insanity in this experiment. Steve normally "volunteered" his subordinates in these risky jaunts into the quantum world, but he was pulling out all the stops on this one. Any other choice was null and void. Tonight it was all or nothing.

Steve reflected for a second. What would Isaac Newton do? He had studied him and knew that Newton would do it and not worry about anything but the experiment. What had impressed Steve was the interaction between Newton and Haley. One day he wanted to write a book about the ancient event of their meeting.

Steve grinned broadly. The truth was that Newton would get out of bed and sometimes just sit there for hours while private revelations weaved themselves in and out of his consciousness. Steve knew he wasn't that smart, and he hoped he never got that distracted; perhaps that would have been dementia instead of intelligence. He was close to getting the sample and Steve might end up turning himself into a pancake, but this was his last chance to go forward. He was well past discussing rhetoric and excuses.

The Institute thought of it as a quantum archaeology experiment: the quest to pull this body out of suspended animation for inspection. This would be the first success of its kind. The war had destroyed all historic DNA and in front of him, surrounded by a blue glow, was his lifelong mission.

Both the Institute and Jade wanted to know what life was like before the War. They wanted the opportunity to ask questions about why the entire array of psychic phenomena had disappeared roughly at the time of Bayou's demise. The Institute also wanted to know why this figure was the last of the great ghost-fighters. Had his father been as impressive as the legends indicated? Why had Bayou been put into suspended animation? Had Mist really died in 2012, the last of the Savage line?

Quirk's report had been distorted by the War, and critical data was lost. It was certain that something momentous had occurred and that Bayou's father had been killed. Bayou disappeared shortly after, followed by Quirk's untimely death. The event had been leaked to the media who thought Bayou had committed suicide right after his father's death; it made for better ratings!

The conspiracy theorists threw out a new conjecture every few years. One speculation was that Bayou had sacrificed himself for mankind: that was why there had been no ghost sightings since his death. Another theory was that Bayou's guitar had consumed him. Therefore he was frozen in another dimension, waiting to escape.

Steve's favorite theory was simply this: no one would ever learn anything more about Bayou Savage until they accessed the guitar. The body was controlled through the guitar. He was now certain that the guitar and pickups held the answer to this legend. The goal of Steve's experiment was to slice off a piece of the guitar—during the nanosecond in which it manifested itself in this dimension. He would then run the piece and see if there was any DNA on the pickup. Steve planned to run the DNA through the Memory Differential he had developed. If there was any DNA, Steve hoped to access it and learn how this person interacted with the environment. He hoped to learn how Bayou's primitive world existed, and how he had reflected with that reality. Also, there might be a chance—a small chance—that instead of accessing the DNA, they might bring Bayou back to this reality. He didn't know for sure what would happen, but he was the main guinea pig tonight.

The tricky part was determining where in time Steve would access Bayou's reality. The problem with this was that he would live out the memory in virtual real time. If Steve could access the DNA, he could do brain fingerprinting—invented and pioneered by the CIA. Of course the procedure had been modified, but it was an old concept. It would set up, at minimum, a test capture to ensure that the measurement of the brain signal would be what the person's memory recognized.

This meant that if Steve only accessed passive memory, he could flash pictures to see if there was a recognition pattern. The association was similar to carbon dating; it could more or less distinguish era recognition of the inhabitant DNA.

One sidespin of that pioneer research was that it had influenced employment practices of the future. It was found that people could learn information skills, but not behavioral traits. People with the right traits learn surprisingly quickly. It totally changed the Human Resource paradigm. Steve was always about the science; he wasn't much of a salesman. He looked around all the while, pacing back and forth. Jade smiled at Steve, sensing his turmoil.

He slowed down and stopped in front of the experiment chair. He returned Jade's smile as he hooked himself to the exoskeleton, which would conduct and flash the memory signals to his brain. If Steve was successful, what could this memory teach him? He was intrigued. All the video recorders were on, and it was approaching ground zero. The recorders captured two signals. He hoped that at least one would work. One would record the signal straight, the second would filter the signal.

No one had ever tried as many variables. Steve didn't even want to think of the odds of this experiment. If it didn't work, he would know that he had pursued the wrong angle for twenty years and would be replaced with the newest chipmaster out there, most likely more of an ass-kisser than he was—someone who knew "politics."

Steve's forehead glistened with sweat; his face held a grim, determined smile. He finally looked up at Brown and gave him a sarcastic nod. "This is what science is all about, Brown; something you wouldn't understand."

Brown looked again at Oswalt, hoping to stop this ridiculous waste of resources. Brown thought that conducting this on Halloween was especially dramatic; he didn't get the opportunistic significance.

At one minute to midnight, Steve was going for Trick-or-Treat pandemonium. He felt a trickle of fear, knowing that logic can distort as well as clarify an experience. Steve affixed the virtual glasses, mouthpiece, and ear buds. The prospect of a treat, rather than a trick, appealed to him greatly in this last minute. Steve was a dead scientist sitting beside his last project, the only one that had ever mattered to him. Bullocks to Brown! He thought, and his blood pressure skyrocketed.

Steve had secretly tried exposure therapy doing what was called the "in-vivo desensitization" technique. He had practiced learning to control his fears and responding in a positive outlook. Basically, emotional self-talk, and it had worked. Steve was prepared. He still had stomach butterflies, but he felt in control. His left-brain kicked in, reviewing the facts and functions; next his right brain kicked in, anticipating the culmination of his dream.

Steve heard the laser locking on and knew that in 10 seconds the sequence would begin. This had to be perfect timing; anything premature could destroy Steve's brain.

Normally, DNA memory cuts had about twelve months of memory condensed down to thirty-six hours. The light shifted and he had one last thought before the laser cut. Whoever this guy was, Steve was going to experience his life. What would he find? What caused the suicide? Who was this person of legend? Who was Bayou Savage? Steve smiled at Jade, hidden behind her shielded translucent barrier. She smiled back and gave him an enthusiastic thumbs-up.

There was a brilliant flash of light, and Steve felt his head implode. His brain opened up and he felt the pain of a knife slashing into his head. He saw images imposed on images—thousands of them. After an eternity, they coalesced into several single images of some kind of old, old room. He felt the wave template of a DNA memory scan kick in. Success and vertigo, he thought to himself, smiling. Again, Steve felt the pain. Some underpinning of the memory hold was engaging. His reflexes told him that something was wrong. He heard a voice in his head. It was interactive. This couldn't be happening! No DNA had a present-tense voice. Steve heard a laugh and felt a frisson of fear. Something was horribly wrong!

The voice sounded as if it were waking up. "I don't know you. Who are you?"

Steve answered the voice. "I'm Steve Johnson, head scientist, Level IV at the Institute." He felt a splitting of his cerebral database.

Steve knew he was being pulled in several different directions. He distinctly knew that he was now incorporeal, like the body in the crypt. He could hear alarms going off all over the place, but he couldn't move. He tried to abort, but couldn't move. He felt hands on his body, things being injected into him. The patient voice came back, and his eyes told him he was still in the old room.

"What do you want, Steve Johnson, head scientist of the Institute?" the voice from nowhere said.

"I...I was trying to access the memory of this body, whom we believe is Bayou Savage, through his DNA," he stuttered. Steve felt fear like he had never known. He was enclosed in this room and no longer felt his body, or anything else.

"Jade, where are you?" Steve yelled manically, feeling as if he was losing control.

"Yes, this is Bayou Savage's body. Why are you trying to access his memory?" the voice asked.

"Why...why the Institute has him as the greatest ghost-fighter of all time," Steve said, frightened and devoid of any logical thought process, "and I want to know: *Who the hell was Bayou Savage?*"

CHAPTER 5

❀

Steve recognized the antiques in front of him. He was in the past, looking at a room through someone else's eyes. He heard a voice inside his mind saying, "I'll show you, Johnson. Open your brain and I will let you into the memories. Remember, though, we only have a few hours; at sunrise the magic will wear off. Be prepared for a hell of ride. Time is short!"

The voice laughed, and Steve felt his personality merging into a dominant DNA memory. He let go and drifted in an amino acid auxiliary functionality, feeling the voice guide him. "Float into the memories and I will guide you actively; just listen, if you want to understand what happened. You have until sunrise to record this. Halloween, you know!"

Steve heard another laugh and felt his brain slashed. "Jade!" he called. He embraced her name, trying to remember who she was. Steve focused on her face as he felt his mind ripped to pieces. Another template was being overlaid onto his own brain. He tried not to fight it. This was what he had wanted, but he found himself fighting it anyway, a self-preservation technique, probably. He hoped like hell the videos were working. "Please, please record this," was his final thought before he slipped away into the memory vortex.

Jade froze; she felt that she had just heard Steve mentally send her a signal. It sounded something like, "Jade, please record this!"

She whipped around, focusing on Steve. The scientists had stabilized his blood pressure, and Steve looked calm in his exoskeleton. The videos were kicking in, but there was some kind of interference. One of the scientists yelled out that they had two tracks coming in.

"That's impossible," said another.

"Unless the quantum brain is still alive!" yelled the first.

Brown yelled, sounding genuinely scared. "Turn the damn thing off! You're killing him." Everyone froze and looked up at the wall screen.

The videos that caught the nanosecond direct feed did show two signals, which was impossible, unless there really were two signals being input. What could be causing the second signal? Several scientists were running around at top speed, trying to discover the cause of the second signal input. If it wasn't artificial, then it was coming straight from the artifact and the body.

Jed voiced his dismay. "This has never happened before. There is no way a dead body can produce a direct variable live input."

Jade looked up at the recording wall again. All the feeds showed the same thing: an antique room, probably dating from around the turn of the century. Jade laughed softly; the bastard had succeeded.

Now, it would be a miracle if he could hold on without frying his brain. Her nurturing instincts told her Steve would make it through, and she realized that her feelings for him were deep. His condition awakened Jade's need for him. She hadn't realized the full depth of her feelings until now. Tears fell down her soft, fragile face. Damn him! She thought. If he dies now, whom will I have those fabulous conversations with? He would never know how precious he was to her. He could synthesize any and every subject without effort. She loved the way Steve could discuss literature, nature, biology, sociology, and history with consummate skill, intelligence, humor, and attention; he could do all that while eating and smiling that idiot smile of his.

Director Oswalt smiled at Jade. "Well, the good news is that the SOB didn't blow up the lab this time." He turned to Jed, ignoring Brown, who was standing beside him. "How's it going? How's he doing?" He had a concerned, curious look on his face.

Jade was happy to see Oswalt supporting Steve on the last leg of this last quest of his. Oswalt carried a lot of clout and had always been open-minded. Everyone admired him, despite his faults. Oswalt was a walking enigma. He had a massive brain for trivia. His main areas of expertise were organization and direction. Many Institute people had tried to get him to teach courses on the subjects, so he had buckled in and done it, until he found that no one actually practiced his advice, and he had stopped. Still, his organizational abilities were the talk of the grapevine and the main reason the Institute was still in business. He knew how to make money. His favorite line was, "It all starts with organization and knowing your people!" Oswalt knew his people!

What most people didn't know was that Oswalt was also an amateur magician and was very practiced with his hands. He could misdirect your eyes and pull off incredible feats, but he would only perform them before a select group of people. Oswalt took over and slalomed through the running scientists. When he got to the videos, he immediately recognized that something was wrong. His natural gifts were manifesting themselves in real time. He touched the monitor where the second signal was registering.

He turned to the scientists surrounding Steve's body and asked, "Is he stabilized?"

"Yes, Director Oswalt," responded Jed, who was monitoring the body. "The coffin is pulsing a conclusive second signal. The problem is its origin; we can't place it." Jed was accustomed to quantum field conditions, but this second input was unexplainable.

Another scientist spoke up, saying, "His body is fine, but his brain is fibrillating."

"Should we abort?" Oswalt could make the tough decisions, and if he thought Steve might lose his life he would shut it down. No one looked up. Oswalt was the Director, after all.

Brown spoke up. "Sir, Steve was meticulous and prepared us ahead of time if something like this occurred. He said if we made successful contact, follow through with it until he expired. He even signed an organ donor certificate." Brown walked over with the donor certificate, gave his best devilish smile, and then slowly walked back over to where he had been standing.

Both monitors displayed the same thing. This meant that she and Steve were experiencing the same visuals in real time. The objectives now were to learn what was slashing into his brain, and to find out where in the quantum world that second input was coming from.

"Relax, Steve," said the voice in his mind. "Here we go, straight into the memories. I'll try to help, but I haven't reviewed this myself. Let's see what happened." Steve's mind froze. He asked a mental question, "Who am I talking with? Bayou, is that you?"

"Relax, Steve; I'm just as confused as you are. Let's see what we have to work with first—answers later."

Steve was confused. No memory scan in history ever talked back. It was normally a fragment download. Ninety-nine percent of the population couldn't afford to do memory scans, only the rich and famous or their lawyers. Most of the middle and lower classes lived and died without a memory review.

Steve thought to himself, "Maybe this person, this Bayou Savage, has the opportunity that no other person has been given. He was alive and able to review his life by his own DNA memory scan.

Steve felt Bayou's memory kick into gear. Jade watched with the rest of the scientists as the videos began to record a voice, along with the room.

"Typical thoughts coming from my atypical brain," Bayou's voice began. Thoughts ran through my head as I tried to fight the tension and the damn heat. "Hey, Johnson, I know you're there. You have the opportunity to review the thoughts and events as recorded. I'll see if I can pull up the best of the scan to answer everyone's questions. Understand that I cannot edit, only choose those critical events most helpful to the Institute." The voice faded in Steve's mind.

Steve heard Bayou's thoughts. Again, he felt shock: no memory scan had ever recorded the real-time thought process. Steve was already feeling over-loaded and helpless to do anything but experience the memory. He said a quick prayer, unconsciously, as he slid into the thought vocalizing itself in his brain. He knew the danger. This memory would become his memory, his body, and his mind.

"As usual," Bayou's voice kicked in, "I had bitten off more than I could chew. My father pulled me into the disastrous scene. Ghosts and guitars—he had pulled me into a whole new world.

"Steve," he heard the mental intruder again, "I have accessed your mind and I'm sorry for the searing sensation. Using the guitar, I understand what you want. The fate was the destiny that the Institute needed. It was the candle that never wanted to be lit.

"Your distortion will abate and I will let you see the life. I will try to explain what is going on as we progress. Steve, let go of your panic. I won't hurt you, and yes, I'm here with you—at least until sunrise. Just relax and discount the bad judgments; the efforts were hard, the events were real.

"We'll start with the first encounter with the guitar, the Bloodstone, the Institute, all the dirty laundry. Remember, you were the one to wake me up. I didn't want this!

"We have a lot to accomplish and only a few hours to do it. Pay attention and be ready for instructions after the memory download!"

Steve felt remorse and desperation in the voice, and for some reason he understood. Something tragic had occurred, and before the night was over there was a plan to accomplish something besides the memory download. "I can access and activate Bayou's neocortex, so hold on."

Steve heard a pause, and then a different tone. A sleepy, irritated voice kicked in. "Okay, Okay, let's rock and roll!"

"Steve, I will take you to the first time Razor fought a ghost with Bayou. I will try to feed you first-person point of view. It's incredible, the stuff you guys wrote. The truth of the story will freak you out." Steve could not reply. He could only listen. He appreciated the fact that he had finally succeeded.

The Bayou Savage! Steve thought to himself. *Either I'm hallucinating or I have hit a grand slam. If I'm comatose and fantasizing, this is the best, most realistic fantasy that I've ever had.* He thought of Jade and what she might be doing. He beamed a thought to her. *Jade, I hope you see and record what I'm about to see.*

Steve's mind caught the feeling of being pulled into a memory. His brain buckled and lost control for a few seconds; his head was splitting from the dynamic tension. He felt that his brain was trying to access too much data, almost like trying to suck peanut butter through a straw.

Then Steve felt like he pushed through some kind of transbrain barrier. His brain felt the imposition of two brains occupying the same space. He was looking through Bayou's eyes. He felt what Bayou felt. He was hungry and scared. *He was Bayou!*

CHAPTER 6

❀

Steve's first look through Bayou's eyes was inside an archaic house, late 20th century. He was conscious, aware of his own identity, but there was a danger that he could lose himself in this mnemonic state. Steve knew that he had just accomplished the most outlandish experiment in quantum history. He had risked everything and finally pushed the right quantum buttons. "At the time, I was trying to think of anything but the disastrous situation Razor had gotten me into." Bayou's voice had a soft melodic ambiance to it.

Jade looked at the monitor and thought, "This is incredible. They were getting a three-dimensional record. This was a first. Normally, a DNA memory scanned recorded some visuals, some audio clips. The video was recording history by looking through the eyes of the subject. All visuals were crystal clear, as was the audio. What dumbfounded Jade was the audio of the conscious mind. This was not possible! She was receiving visual, auditory, and first person consciousness.

Jade felt dizzy and noticed that all the observing scientists were sitting on the floor or perched on something. It was affecting all of them the same way. Jade also knew that this was the experience of her lifetime. If what she suspected were true, they would have an actual historical real-time recoding of Bayou Savage, with his own submerged thoughts providing insight to his motives. Jade whispered a quick but heartfelt prayer, "Thank you, God!" Bayou's death would finally be explained—a mystery that had intrigued her for too long.

Jade heard Bayou's conscious voice kick in as she observed the scene. It sounded like he was talking to someone; but no, it couldn't be! There was no way he could be giving a firsthand narrative to Steve. She felt a cold chill; there could be no way—unless the DNA had generated a mystical imperative scan. Could the second input be the ghost of Bayou Savage?

Bayou's voice bounded through the speakers. "As one of the Institute's part-time brand new psychic investigators, also known as a field agent, I wasn't sure what to expect. I did figure this situation was too quiet. The waiting was evidently part of the job, but if something is going to happen, it will probably happen when least expected. Times like this, or any time I'm waiting, well, it just kills me. Waiting gets on my nerves.

Jade's mind whirled.

Bayou's voice continued, "Right here, right now, I'm about to have my first psychic experience. Okay, any minute now, I'm about to have my first psychic experience. Come on, ghost, show up, and let's get this over with. It's closing time, time for all ghosts to drink up and go home. Come on, Bayou. I said to myself, "Be patient, be patient!"

Steve, Jade, the scientists, and Oswalt all felt the mystical bond being created between the watcher and the watched. They were all becoming Bayou. It overpowered them. No one noticed the reddish hue emanating from the coffin. Bayou's voice gripped them as he talked to himself. "Damn, what a long night! It's too quiet, too quiet. No noise here but the creaking of the house. Off in the distance I could see this weird kind of lightning that happened on warm summer nights. The light seeped through the curtains, casting grotesque caricatures on the walls and floor. The patterns held an eerie fascination for me. Fate was coming home to roost. Pathological, I know, but the night and its creatures were out and about. The wait was having an effect.

"I put my brain into the old Bayou-random-chaos-thought maneuver. This is a freewheeling creative association I use without regard for logic or time. The motif is a stream-of-consciousness awakening with a total random linear trance stance. Why am I doing the ole Bayou random maneuver? Because I'm scared; it's not normal for me to want to commit suicide with my father.

"Razor's revelation to me concealed a truth. This was a suicide mission. My brain had an adrenaline buzz going. I asked myself again, why am I getting into this mess? My father is a unique man—a hard man. One thing about Razor: if we die here, we will die fast. He doesn't pussyfoot around."

As Jade was videoing a first-hand report of the famous Razor Savage, incredulity flashed across her features and began to affect her. Jade could exhume history directly tonight; she felt the excitement course through her and ignite her. Razor had died a hero, but no one knew much about him, except through Quirk's cryptic reports.

Bayou's voice dropped into a whisper as he spoke to himself. "I need to calm down. I'll use my favorite stress-reduction technique; it comes in handy at times like this. It's like emotional judo to get my mind off the current circumstances. I call it free-floating vortex. If I think hard enough, I don't allow for emotional distress. I have a stack of my favorite questions; the secret is to pick one and free-flow with it.

"For example, the thoughts that were floating through my head now were what worked best to get my mind off this stress. Thoughts like, *Why did the most precious legacy of the ancient Greeks—their Greek Athenian music—not survive historically?* It was their most remarkable accomplishment, but not an original trace survived. I also wondered what the biblical King David's music sounded like. His psalms—the words—survived, but not the music. The Bible has him as God's musician, and I would have loved to hear the jams he played. Information like that always intrigued me—the data that we don't find in our regular history books. Those are the types of things that I occupy my mind with.

"I heard crashing noises upstairs and felt the air getting colder. Interesting, the way history works. I kept thinking of other random thoughts while waiting for the oncoming chaos. The air was freezing, and I saw my breath wafting away in a frozen fog."

The observers in the lab could see the white cloud of Bayou's exhaled breath.

Bayou's voice continued, shaking slightly; the cold was starting to have an effect. "Ah, too much time. How did I get here? I rubbed my hands to keep warm and had one of those late-at-night intuitive stupors, trying to figure out how this crazy house got this way. So I sit here on this old barstool in this stupid haunted house. My anxieties were not quite at the obsessive stage, but they were getting close. I suddenly heard what sounded like a miniature explosion. The window to my left exploded outward. Not a shred of glass remained. I looked around in disbelief, but nothing was there. I tensed, waiting for the next event. Nothing happened. I heard Dad, old Razor yell, "Don't worry. It's nothing!"

"Easy for him to say, I thought.

"The house was restricted to humans. That's what the Institute—the psychic investigation agency in all this mess—calls houses not safe for human habitation. The owner's narrative went something like this: He bought the house, then as he and his family started the moving process, weird happenings occurred—unexplained events, like temperature extremes and objects levitating across the room. Then mist creatures with heads the size of pumpkins started showing up.

"Like I said, weird happenings. Most people would sell and move immediately. I believed the part about temperature extremes; I couldn't handle much more of this."

CHAPTER 7

❀

Jade caught on that Steve was somehow hearing Bayou's inner dialogue and that a voice was somehow explaining past events to Steve. Bayou's inner voice sounded desperate. The tone was tight and anxious, like he was narrating, while waiting for disaster to take place at any moment.

"Our owner did not think or react, in my opinion, the way normal people would. He thought these happenings were peripheral and tried to live with it. Our owner didn't care, but his wife did. She investigated, wanting to know why the house was for sale; she found out that it was said to be haunted. That's when she decided to divorce the idiot she'd married. That action brought him to the Institute."

Everyone on both ends of the quantum time frame laughed. Steve surfaced enough to realize that some things never change. But he understood, too, that there had at one time actually been a bona fide psychic phenomenon. Steve thought that idiots were operational across the span of history. The good news was that his bashing headache had decreased. Steve liked Bayou. He was intelligent, scared, and sounded absolutely normal. He knew it was a first impression, but Bayou seemed to be a likable, normal person. Of course this was before the guitar and Bloodstone. What had happened to Bayou?

Steve no longer thought of him as Bayou Savage, but as a real person caught up in real-time events. He sounded more intelligent than someone who had lived so long ago. His decisions and thoughts sounded rational.

Bayou continued. "Somehow, the Institute was contacted and they in turn contacted my father. My father, Razor Savage, retired from the rubber plant, and secretly worked for the Institute when he had the opportunity. All of this covert history I have just recently found out. It was floating through my hot and tense mind as I sat there, waiting for whatever was going to happen.

"Another window next to me exploded. Again, the eerie quiet resounded after the explosion. There was only one more window in the house. Dad yelled, 'Don't worry, it's nothing!'"

Steve, Jade, and everyone else in the room felt the tension, along with Bayou. Where was Razor?

Bayou continued. "'*Nothing* doesn't blow the windows out of the house, Dad.' But Dad sounded like he was setting up equipment so I'd be cool. My nerves were tighter than the bottom-gauge 'E' string being stretched by Nugent."

It occurred to Steve and Jade that this must have been early in Bayou's three-year career. He sounded surprisingly uneasy.

Bayou's voice sounded more and more scared. He continued in a tense voice that was reminiscent of a trapped victim. "While waiting, I started one of those famous television *Kung-Fu* series David Caradine flashbacks. Sometimes I used another stress technique. When in the middle of a stressful event, I would flash back to the history of a current event.

"It was just two weeks ago that Dad let me in on his little part-time work secret. It was one of those rare instances when I should have known something was coming. Dad called me up and asked what was going on in my life and if I could meet him for breakfast. I said 'ok,' and we agreed on where to meet.

"He asked, 'Son, how's business?' I made the usual noises; my job as a Quality Consultant was going great, but right now was a slow time."

Steve and Jade both registered the remark. Bayou Savage had been a Quality Consultant! It shocked both of them. Steve never thought of Bayou Savage as anything but a ghost-fighter. It was like discovering that Jesus was a carpenter before He took up a public ministry. What did a Quality Consultant actually do? Steve didn't know, but made a note to himself, if he survived this, to research it.

Jade had a different reaction. She knew exactly what a Quality Consultant did: Analyze, train, and consult systems optimization. If Bayou understood system mentality, inputs, throughputs, outputs, and a feedback loop, he would have been a natural strategist. He'd have been a natural problem solver with those skills.

"Razor asked if I was playing guitar with anyone right now, and I said 'No.' Since the divorce, and with Mist getting ready to go to college again, I was trying to spend as much time with her as I could. Mist had the philosophy that you don't *have* a great life; you *make* a great life. She went through life with bank shots versus straight-ins.

"Razor said he understood, as only a thoughtful father could, and then we talked about the nature of women. We had a dedicated routine as one of our father-son favorite topics. It's interesting to note that in our conversations, we were never irresponsible in our dealings, and we both played the tragic, noble role well. Dad launched into his speech number twelve about how I should have never married a damn Yankee. Dad honestly believed that my unfortunate run of luck with women had to be blamed 100% on them being Yankees!

"He believed that I courted Yankee women just to bring both of us misery, and that marrying a Yankee constituted an extreme form of masochism. He believed that hopping over the geographical lines—which I have done—intruded and drifted into Tabasco mentality minefields, because Northern women just don't understand the synaptic minds of the South. But I was always with women from the North, due to my geographical location, and I found his assumptions to be false—amusing, but false. I found that the problem was not with where the women were from, but with my own insecurities.

"But Dad liked the current Yank I was seeing, and coming from him, that was practically an endorsement."

Jade smiled to herself. Bayou was a lover! She sensed in him an incurable romantic. She really wanted to see his face; the videos showed only the view of a room with shattered glass and his cold white exhalations. Jade understood the references to the demographics, which were normal in any culture. What surprised her was how close the father and son actually were. Was that normal before the War?

Bayou's voice kept reminiscing. "We always talked about women, since I'm not really into fishing, which was his big love. So Razor said, 'No woman, and Mist getting ready to go to college again. What are you going to do with yourself?'

"Mist was the love of my life, ripening every day. She shielded me from her yo-yo bouts with life when she could, but like every parent, I tried to engage her and give her the benefit of not doing it the hard way. I felt that I would stay here five more minutes and then leave. Dad would have to find a warmer place to fight ghosts if he wanted me involved. Thinking back to that conversation, I remembered the ground we had covered.

"'I don't know, Dad, maybe sapphire hunting, my current passion, might just make me rich.'

'Well, son, sapphires are a lot of fun and our ancestors spent a lot of money and time prospecting, but it seems that our family isn't worth a shit at finding anything buried in the ground. Now that brings me to something I need to tell you. I'm 70 years old and might possibly be here for the next 30. We Savages have a little something handed down to us that is important to your future.'

Jade surfaced enough to grasp this bit of monologue. Bayou was into stones. This meant he understood geology and the lapidary sciences. This was significant. This meant the email she uncovered was legitimate and trustworthy. Her last thought before fading back into the vid was of the beautiful color of a natural star sapphire and how it matched certain people's eyes.

"Well," Bayou continued, "this was news to me, since I knew the only basic heirloom handed down was a perpetual cycle of fun, bills, and wanderlust, so I had no idea what in the hell he might be talking about. Also passed on was an antipathy toward the IRS and a fear of senility.

"'Listen,' he said, 'I have this 1953 Fender Esquire guitar. The neck broke, and I replaced it with a sacred piece of wood. The wood came from Europe and was from a friend of your grandfather Savage.'

"The Esquire is a great guitar. Dad always played Fender, but he also had a cool Gretch hollow body, a Gibson SG, and numerous other fine guitars through the years. He could never afford a Les Paul, and we both thought it was a heavy guitar. He liked my Parker P-38 because it was lightweight. Out of all his guitars, he claimed that the Fender was some kind of holy relic. I liked Fenders, but appreciated the extra two frets on the Gibson's.

"As I waited for the punch line, I saw that he was 100% serious. 'You are joking, aren't you, Dad?' My father was anything but nonchalant. I had given him my *don't-walk-slowly-through-the-woods-because-you-are-nuts* look. He stared hard, while maintaining that demanding old patriarchal look.

"'No, listen, son, I'm not sure how much longer I can keep doing this investigator job, and I need you to take my place. If the guitar works for me, then it should work for you. Are you with me? I'm no longer asking; I'm telling you!'

"'Whoaaa,' I exclaimed. "Dad, please explain to me what the hell you're talking about; go slow for a minute. You know how you like to rush, and this sounds pretty complicated, okay?'

"'Well, it's pretty simple,' he said, in his *I'll-try-to-slow-down-so-the-rest-of-you-idiots-can-catch-up* tone. 'I work for and receive periodic phone calls from this group named—are you ready for this—*The Institute.*

"'The Institute is a group of professional skeptics and Ghostbusters who are transnational. Anytime a genuine psychic occurrence surfaces in this neck of the woods, they call me and I go investigate with this bag of Radio Shack electronic spy stuff and the guitar. 90% of the time it's just weird coincidence and has nothing to do with genuine psychic phenomenon. The other 10% of the time, I really need the guitar! The guitar protects me from real psychic phenomenon and has saved my life more than once or twice! Oh, and on a side note—ghosts don't know any nationalities, or at least they don't recognize any boundaries that I've seen.'

"With that he sat back and acted like this short speech just totally explained everything and there couldn't possibly be any questions or misunderstandings. I wondered, of course, what's not to understand?

"As I looked at him, I also wondered how much strain he had been under lately. He looked normal, healthy, and sane. So, I asked in my *is-this-the-first-sign-of-Alzheimer's-or-stroke-manifestation* voice, 'Who do you think you are, Dad?'

"'Damn it, son, quit acting like an idiot! I don't have time for you to sit there thinking that I've lost my damn mind!'

"One thing I always loved about my dad was that he could swear with flair. Exasperated, he held up his age-spotted hands.

"'Now this is serious; listen to me. There's this haunted house—what we call a *delta*—right here in Waynesville, North Carolina. It's been reported to the Institute, and Quirk—the coordinator in charge—wants us to investigate. I need you to go with me. So what are you doing Saturday night?'

"'Nothing, Dad. Nothing that I can think of right now,' I said. 'But let me ask a few questions. If you're serious about this investigation, what do we do, what do we bring, what time do I need to show up? Give me all the logistics. Now, tell me about the guitar; you've got my curiosity aroused! And Dad, do you want me to bring the Martin or any of my other guitars?'

"As I said this, I wondered if I needed to put new strings on any of them. One of my lucky attributes is that I don't sweat. That is great for the guitar. I've played with some guitar players who sweat, and it corrodes the strings so fast they have to be replaced every week. My strings can last up to four months.

"'Well, no,' he motioned as he talked. 'The only guitar that works is this one with the sacred wood neck. Your guitar would be as worthless as tits on a bull.' He paused and said, 'Now, let's get on with it. If you don't pay close attention to what I'm about to tell you, then I guarantee you'll live to regret not listening.

"'The guitar has some sort of magical protection that lets the player boost his PSI energies to a viable force field against real psychic negative forces. I'm not real sure of all the technical mumbo-jumbo; you can check with the Institute for that. But put it like this: if the phenomenon is not artificial, then you better pray that guitar is close.

"'It has saved my sanity and ass quite a few times, because when the shit hits the fan, that Fender Esquire is the only thing that I have found that gives you any protection. A breather, so to speak, so you can collect your thoughts against the weird abominations out there. Now, be ready at 11 P.M. Saturday and I'll pick you up in the Chevy S-10. Unless it's raining; if it rains, I'll be in the Crown Victoria.'

"'Okay, Dad, I'll be ready. Do I need to bring anything?' I had a sinking, deep-down premonition that there was no escaping this weird musical fate. Plus, I hoped I wouldn't have to buy anything. Lately I'd had a serious case of financial cancer. If he needed me to buy anything, I would need a dose of financial chemo first.

"'Now we were there. Damn, it was time I got out of there. I was frozen with fear. It was almost midnight, and I was sitting here in this old bar someone had turned into a house, with my crazy father in another room, waiting to fight some supernatural powerhouse. With my luck, if there were a ghost, it'd be the Mike Tyson of ghosts. I was trying to think of anything I had read through the years that would provide me ghost diplomatic immunity. Nothing came to mind. Time was spiraling inside. I kept looking at the last remaining window, expecting it to blow. Whatever encounter would follow was beyond anything I could imagine.

"Then I heard it! The last window blew out, and next came a noise that sounded like a damn freight train coming right through the living room. I jumped over the couch and looked for the Bose sound system that was producing this monster effect. I heard my father yelling something in the next room and started toward him. As I ran into the room, I noticed all of this monitoring equipment and an instrument panel that looked like the cockpit of 747 in a mid-flight. There were different panels lighting up, and bells and buzzers going full volume.

"'Shit!' he yelled. 'It's worse than I thought.'

Steve was looking at the famous Razor Savage through Bayou's eyes, and it was an emergency. He could sense Bayou's mental and physical state. Razor looked about 70 years old, six feet tall, and around 230 pounds. He had thin white hair and a round, commanding face. Steve looked hard at him and saw no fear; he reminded Steve of Jade. They both had that strong aura of *get on with it.*

Jade stared hard at the video. Razor Savage looked something like—and yet nothing like—she had imagined. She had been prepared by listening to Bayou reminisce about his personality, but putting that personality with this figure put her out of sync. Razor was old, that was obvious, but his energy and presence were incredible. He was a warrior, ready to engage in a do-or-die battle. Time froze, and then she heard Bayou's voice and saw Razor look up at him.

"'I hear you,'" Bayou yelled back. "'How serious is worse? I knew something was going down and that we were in trouble.'

"'Dad, where is that noise coming from? Where's the back door? Let's get out of here!'

"Razor ignored me. 'It's a temporal psychic real-to-life stuff hitting the fan epicenter ghost! Get over here quick! We have about'—he glanced at his watch as the lights erupted into a disco show—'twenty-two seconds before all hell breaks loose and erupts!'

"I had never seen my father scared. It wasn't that he was scared now, but more that he was moving at hyper speed that got my full attention.

"'What should I do?' I yelled, trying to raise my voice over the airplane volume that was only increasing.

"'Stay next to me and don't get beyond the locus of control.'

Steve, Jade, and all the Institute's personnel present sensed the aura of command behind Razor's orders. They felt Bayou's fear and Razor's pure, controlled anger. Through Bayou's eyes they saw the guitar they had seen and heard about their entire lives as it was put into action.

The coffin was now emitting a reddish field that encased the room. Everyone in the room was motionless, waiting for the next event.

Bayou's voice came through loud and proud. "The next few seconds I will never forget. He slung the old 53 Fender Esquire across his shoulder, plugged in the cable, hit the *on* switch, and struck a G bar chord in all of three seconds. He looked over, flashed one of his devilish grins and said, 'Hold on; this is going to be a big one!' As I watched, the guitar's yellow body and plate started flashing, burning bright lights, and the machine heads began to glow.

"He looked incredible. Lights flashed all around us, like an electric aurora borealis. I stood there while the air pressure kept getting heavier, waiting, as if there was something big about to happen, waiting for the right moment.

"I glanced at my watch, exactly midnight. My head was killing me. It was like all the oxygen had left the room and bright lights were swirling around my eyes. I saw streaks of phantomlike patches and felt like gravity was pulling me down. I felt depravity all around me. At the moment I thought I was going to pass out, I heard a sound I had been raised on—the sweet sound of that ole Fender kicking in.

"On my right I saw Dad, with teeth clenched, holding onto the guitar. He was chording with his left hand and turning up the volume with his little finger, while his thumb fingerpicked. The refrain from *Eight More Miles to Louisville* was coming through loud and clear.

"Dad laughed and started picking faster and faster; lights began to stream out of the guitar. Tricky tonalities and immaculate dynamics, accented by his fear and excitement, held me totally mesmerized. I had seen him play, but never this fast—never. It was like Eddie Van Halen and Merle Travis, merged with a little bit of Joe Maphis on the side.

"The lights coming through the guitar were going nova. I heard the most awful crying and moaning coming from everywhere in the remaining darkness. One massive explosion boomed after another. Black billowing smoke seemed to surround his amp, and I could see orange flames coming off the guitar, like polychromatic lightning bolts.

"Flying debris filled the room. Dad sounded like he had done a line of super crack or something, the way he was tearing up the fret board. It sounded like musical gunfire with the ghosts wailing for release.

"I couldn't tell if the debris was material or ectoplasm. All I knew was that this room was under a relentless avalanche of screaming Fender assault, and it sounded better than anything I had ever heard in my life. The force and beauty, the notes, were all demolishing the crap out of the ghosts. My ears began to register a letup of the tension.

"'Take that, you son of a bitch! Go back to hell and tell your master, Lucifer, the master musician, that I hope he enjoys the licks!' With that, I heard an implosion—or explosion—that rocked what was left of my head completely off. I laughed hysterically.

"*Was that a real noise I heard? How were Dad and I still alive? Was this a dream? Where was I? Did I tell Mist where I was going?* Those were my last conscious thoughts before I passed out."

CHAPTER 8

❀

Blank blue space was on the video. Time stood frozen until Jade heard Oswalt yell at full volume, "How are the bodies?" Jade heard people yelling at each other and saw peripheral movement. She checked the monitors and saw that the videos were still recording. Perspiration covered Steve's brow; his arched body was now relaxing. He looked yellowish, and Jade could see that the battle had taken a toll on him. The cardiac contact monitor moved to within a quarter centimeter from the actual emergency zone. If Steve survived this encounter, he would be sore as hell and probably have a god-awful migraine.

Jed and one of the physicians stood by Steve's motionless body. The physician was wiggling Steve's toes and Jed was rubbing his body. Steve remained in a trance, not moving, barely breathing. Jade knew that Steve's options were limited: either he would live or not. If there were going to be other battles after this, Jade didn't think he would survive, especially not in the psyche of Bayou. Bayou was too emotional.

Steve had the general logical mind of a good scientist, and this emotional onslaught was a masterpiece of affective domain on his logical mind. If Steve lived through this, how would he emerge? Jade understood that he was at an emotional ground zero. It was affecting her, and she had a tough constitution. She could see other people in the room evacuating.

The video monitor flickered, and all eyes turned toward it. Everyone in the room suddenly felt hungry. Jade saw that the record buttons were still recording, and she relaxed. Looking up at the screen, she inhaled deeply and felt Bayou's memory take over again. Her last thought was how real the videos were. She felt the mental gridlock slip back into her head and smelled food.

"'Wake up, Bayou! Here's some coffee, bacon, eggs, grits, and homemade biscuits and gravy!'

"Man oh man, it smelled fantastic. I opened my eyes. It looked good, and I sure was hungry, for some odd reason. Breakfast controlled and restricted my opening movements. Then it hit me. I was in my bed with my clothes on and Dad looked scared.

"'Kind of had me worried there, Sport, but eat this and you'll feel better!' Like most parents in the south, Dad believed there was no problem that could not be solved with the intake of grits and gravy. Right now I believed in his cure-all solution. 'I think you are in a little bit of shock, so eat up, relax, and we'll talk.'

""'What time is it?' I asked.

"'Oh, about six,' he said.

"'A.M. or P.M.?'

"'A.M., son. You've been out like a light for about five and a half hours. How do you feel?'

"'Loquacious,' I said. Seeing his puzzled look, I laughed and said, 'It means talkative, Dad.'

"He smiled. My normal modus operandi was to use a big word to see if my brain was still functioning. 'I don't know, Dad; I feel weird. Exactly what happened last night? Whatever happened, I believe you now, about all the psychic investigation stuff. I feel like a firsthand participant in one of those action-suspense pictures.'

"'Well, son, like I told you, to make it short and sweet, I do this as a side gig. I got this holy wood, made this guitar, and fight ghosts. How is that for K.I.S.S.?'

"K.I.S.S. was my dad's shortcut for saying keep it short and sweet.

"'Well, Dad, sounds cool to me, and I think your guitar playing was the best I've ever heard. I just have a few questions. First of all, why do I feel like somebody strapped a C4 explosive to my brain? Are you a volunteer martyr for this Institute? I mean, it was exhilarating, watching the pyrotechnics, but if I have this right, you going into a *real* haunted house with just a *magic* guitar is equivalent to wetting your finger and sticking it in a light socket. It's suicide! We could have been blown to smithereens!'

"My body started to grow tense. It grew tenser as I started replaying the events. As I relived the events, I was still surprised to find myself alive.

"'What went down when you played tonight? I've never seen you play that fast, with that efficiency. I mean, you are a great guitar player, but where did you get that speed?'

"'That's the weirdest part, son. I believe what happens is that when the holy wood makes contact with the evil—whatever it is—something happens and I just hang on for the experience. I don't really think about it, I just let it happen. It's like I pickpocket all the great pickers before me, unconsciously. The Institute has a section called the Meta-analysis Unit trying to figure it out.'

"'Dad, I am sure there is a quantum connection. The energy must be coming from somewhere, and the thought I have is a quantum connection. It's a pretty solid theory that has been proven.'

"Well, my father—he's not into theory; he's into what he calls reality. I remember one time, when one of my former spouses was arguing about creation versus evolution, Dad drove up, listened to the conversation, and then stated—in a very clear *Ross Perot–like* manner—'Why in the hell are you arguing about something you can't prove? I mean, the only way you can prove it is to get a time machine and go back about 5 million years. What a bunch of bullshit! Why don't you argue about how your earth bank is eroding away, affecting the foundation, and what to do about that?'

"Dad always delivered those short sermonnettes in an unbelievably loud and anathematizing fashion, so listening to him talk about the reasoning of how the guitar worked sounded about right for him.

Jade tried to move her hand to the remote to signal a tracking mark on the video, but she found that her hand wouldn't move. She tried again; her hand had lost its manageability. She wasn't scared; she knew the cause.

Everyone who was still in the room was surrounded and inundated by a red iridescent glow. A small part of her brain understood that this was the first psychic experience manifested in her lifetime.

Jade hoped that Steve had not thrust them all into a Pandora 's box. Jade knew that if everything broke down now, there would be many years' worth of dissecting. The relationship between Razor and Bayou was incredible. Jade smiled and wondered what Razor had been like in his younger days. He was hell-on-wheels at 70, and capable of inflicting hell on the paranormal world, yet didn't appear to believe in it. He was a dichotomy.

Bayou appeared to be a somewhat myopic ally of Razor. He was bright, practiced a doctrine of family value, and possessed a wry wit.

Bayou continued, "For example, Dad's basic beliefs are that politicians should only be elected for one term—then they might actually get something done. Or, as he says, it will take the crooked bastards two years to get really crooked and might actually get something done. He also believes that elected officials, law enforcement, etc., should serve twice as long a sentence as the criminals that are caught—if the criminal is released and commits another crime."

"Two other beliefs he gave regular institutional speeches about were a strong justification of capital punishment and euthanasia. Both are perfectly reasonable in his mind. There is little room for flexibility in Razor Savage's value system. As we say in quality, he really hugs the control mean. According to the laws of nature, Bayou knew that if you add all the variables in a situation and divide by the number of variables, you get a mean. This observation of an average helped Bayou survive, by understanding the predictability of a situation based upon the average. Razor had the habit of taking a small amount of observations and coming to an instant conclusion.

"'Dad, let me ask you this another way. Does the guitar always work like that? I mean, does it speed you up, shoot the light out, the pyrotechnics show? It looks like a big mystery to me, but how do you feel, for example, when all this is going on?'

"'To be honest with you, son, I don't think about it, I'm so busy fighting for my life. I'm not thinking about how I'm feeling. The Institute sends out this crap I am supposed to read, but it's all Greek to me. They ask the same questions.'

"I could hear the disgust in his voice as he said this. I didn't have to be a mind reader, either, to know what he was thinking. He was thinking, *who gives a cornbread shit about how I feel, or should be feeling? That's not important!*

"'I smiled. 'Let me see what they sent you, Dad,' I said, as he reached into his pocket and pulled out a folded piece of paper.

"It was an article summary from a neuroscience magazine, a study of musicians' brains, and it found a strong relationship between musical ability and a part of the brain called the Heschl's gyrus, which was involved in processing sound. This area of the brain has a much larger volume of gray matter, and also has a stronger activation with musicians than with nonmusical people. Dad was getting impatient and angry, just looking at the article. I could tell from years of knowing him that what he wanted was a self-defrosting memo that had practical advice versus what he considered complex 'useless' information. I could read his mind again.

"His thought pattern went something like this: *Okay, Institute, I'm fighting the ghost and I stop in the middle of the battle and say, Excuse me, ghost, but did you happen to know that the Heschl's gyrus in my brain is larger than most people because I am a musician? What do you think of that? Does that make you want to quit or just kill yourself out of envy?*

"Was there any maintenance in this guitar-activation ritual? I probed. I could tell he was getting angry at what he considered a stupid question. He was probably wondering, for the millionth time, if I was really his offspring. 'Dad, do you know that when the—I guess, whatever it is, the evil ghost thing—kicks in, you do incredible finger work on the guitar? I mean it's unlike anything I've ever seen or heard before. The songs you played I recognized, but not the speed. The licks were light speed, the dynamics a blur, but I recognized them. I mean, Wow, you were incredible! How did it feel? Could you feel what you were doing? Was there a power surge in your brain?

"'Damn, how many frivolous questions are you going to ask?'

"'Okay, how about this one. Did you know what you were doing as far as the blistering speed you were cranking?'

"'Are you asking me, did I get blisters?'

"'No, Dad. I was asking, did you know how fast you were picking?' But I did wonder, now that he mentioned it, if he got blisters.

"'Well, son, yes and no. I felt the good power—that's what I figure it was—kick in at the first lick, and then it seemed like the guitar glued itself to me. The harder I played, the more asses I kicked. Plain and simple! It's no big deal on how it worked; it works, period. Look, we can discuss all that later, Bayou. It's time for you to take over.'

"'I haven't heard of anybody in the organization that has the ability to do what this guitar can do. I'll be honest with you. The only way I discovered it was when I was about sixteen and was challenged to spend the night in the old haunted house up in Upper Fines Creek,' Dad continued. 'I did it to get ten dollars, which was a lot of money back then. Plus, being born on Friday the thirteenth, either you are superstitious or not superstitious at all. I've always been an *I'll-believe-it-when-I-see-it* type, so I thought, *Why not make ten dollars?* So I went up there with Dink and AJ and took my rifle and my Fender with me. I had just made a new neck for it because your Aunt Edna broke my original neck over Lois's head during a fight we had while Mom and Dad had gone to town.'

"'So I grabbed this antique block of oak Dad had gotten from some gypsy friend of his—I think he was from Wales—from out in the barn and cut out a neck. I grooved out the frets, replaced the machine heads, and restrung it. Back then you did not have a guitar shop. If you wanted something fixed, you fixed it yourself.'

"'I remember thinking that Dad, your grandfather, would get mad, because he was thinking of making a gun rack with it. I was with him when he bought it over in Asheville and we both thought the old gypsy friend had a few screws loose. He claimed that it was the wood that a Welsh saint had been martyred on and that it was holy. Dad didn't care; he just felt sorry for the old man and appreciated the oak wood.'

Thus started the actual history of the artifact; Steve thought feeling like he was still immersed in molasses and feeling a sense of pride in knowing that he was actually fulfilling his life's dream. He hoped Jade was seeing, experiencing and recording all this.

Then he freaked, who was this Jade person he was thinking about? He wildly fought to regain his identity as he felt himself being drawn back into his memories.

CHAPTER 9

❀

"'Anyway, I went to spend the night in that old house and was pretty sure it was a joke until about 4 A.M. when all hell broke loose. I was sleeping in the living room when I heard an awful shriek coming from the loft. I looked and saw an old lady and three kids floating in the air about five feet in front of me. I'll be honest—I screamed for about a second and grabbed the gun and pointed it right at them. My instinct was that this was either a hell of a ghost or a hell of a prank, and I knew it was going to be the last time who—or whatever it was—tried to scare me. The old lady and kids were glowing this sick yellow color and were pointing at me, laughing and floating closer.

"Then I felt—for the first time, and have felt it many times since then—that atmospheric ear pressure increase and the beginning of a migraine headache. I pointed the gun and shot, not caring about anything being a prank; I just wanted to kill or stop this damn nightmare. I remember thinking if I survived this, next time I'd bring a shotgun, at least a 12 gauge, because these ghosts were going to get me before I could get them.

"'I shot four times straight into the old lady and she just laughed and said, in this otherworldly voice, 'Kill me, Yankee, kill my grandkids; now I will kill you. I will avenge what you did to them!' They kept coming, floating right through the rifle blasts. I knew right damn there I was in a boatload of trouble.

"'I yelled, 'What the hell you talking about, old lady? I'm from here, I'm no Yankee; get away from me!' It was then that I swung the rifle right through them. If there had been any doubts about them being ghosts or not, it was resolved then. They kept approaching, and then stopped. For no reason, they stopped. I was thinking, *these damn ghosts are a preset pattern, because they don't even know that I'm not a damn Yankee.*

"'I'm going to die for something I didn't even do. I could not figure out how they were going to kill me, but make no mistake, I knew that someone was not going to make it out of there alive—and I had a pretty good clue on who that somebody was going to be! I looked down and saw that they had stopped in front of the guitar. They looked like they were in pain.

"'I know it was only about thirty seconds, but it seemed like about thirty minutes. I reached down and grabbed the guitar and went to swing it through them, when in my hurry I accidentally strummed the bottom three strings. The sound sent what looked like miniature lightning bolts out the neck straight into the ghosts. The ghosts wavered a few seconds and then seemed to shrink; the glow was definitely weaker. I swung the base of the guitar through the ghosts without any effect, and they appeared to be coming back.

"'I dropped back and tried to rethink what about the guitar had worked before. Time was running out, and these ghosts were in a mood to kick my young ass by suppertime. It was then that I did the first smart thing I had done all night. I held the neck of the guitar toward the ghosts, remembering some old legend about the effect of silver bullets on vampires and werewolves. Maybe there was some silver in the guitar strings that was acting like a force field. The neck hurt them, or at least appeared to hurt them. For the next few minutes they tried to surround me and I held them off with the neck. A ray of dawn's light appeared through the windows, and the ghosts disappeared. I felt the ear pressure die down after they left.

"'I collapsed, lay down, and thought, *let me grab my rifle. These damn ghosts can have this house and all the damn Yankees they want—have a big Yankee party for all I care. As a matter of fact, invite all the Yankees down and let them have at them all. I don't give a shit; just let me get out of here.*

"'Then, very aggressively, I picked up my blanket and went out to kick some ass of the friends who had tried to get me killed.'

"'Dad showed that grim smile of his. It took me a while to recover from that, and I thought about what had happened for a long time. It all had to do with the neck—and what about those lightning bolts? I tried without success to get the guitar to duplicate what had happened that night. I even went into a graveyard at midnight to see if I could get it to do the lightning bolts again. I just could not figure it out and knew the only way was to go back into that damn house.

"'So, about four months after that, I voluntarily decided to do it again. You'll laugh, but I brought a 12-gauge shotgun with real shells, not just buckshot. I also brought a four-foot-long Southern rebel flag from one of those tourists' places, and I brought my guitar. I wanted them damn ghosts to know where the hell I came from.

"'At four A.M., just like last time, the fireworks began. I was scared shitless when the old lady and kids appeared, floating in midair, just like before. Being the redneck that I am, I fired both damn barrels of the twelve gauges at point-blank range into the ghosts. The recoil threw me back, and I looked up just in time to hear their opening monologue.

"'Kill me, Yankee, kill my grandkids! Now I will kill you. I will avenge what you did!'

"'The shotgun peppered and ripped everything apart except—you guessed it—those damn ghosts. It was like a bad repeating nightmare. They kept coming at me, hovering about eight feet off the ground. I felt a hellacious headache approaching, and that ear pressure hurt worse than before. This time there was no hesitation. I grabbed the base of the guitar, and out of panic thrust the neck at the approaching ghosts. They stopped and actually changed their facial expressions. Then I quickly reversed the guitar in a half-assed playing position. I just wanted to strum a chord quickly, and then put the neck back on them in case I was wrong about my theory.

"'It was incredible. I mean it was really the damnedest thing I've ever felt. I hit a G chord and I felt the entire world explode as this blue-green flash came out of the neck. The ghost shrieked and I hit it again and again. Now I was crazy. I thought, *now it's time to pick and grin, girls, ghosts, and boys.* I screamed out and kept playing that G chord like my hands were glued to the neck. I beat the hell—or heaven, now that I think about it—out of that guitar. I thought surely to God that I would break every string off.

"'The ghosts screamed. They started to pulsate and began to fade with every lick—and then nothing. I felt miniature implosions all around me. After a minute there were no ghosts left that I could see. I looked down, saw the guitar starting to—I guess, un-glow and return to normal. But that was then, and this is now. Bayou, pick up that guitar and let's get down to business!'

The videos faded to blue. The immobility was gone. Whatever mind-lock had been in place was now gone. Everyone was in mental shell shock and motion returned slowly. Director Oswalt went into his autocatalytic process of organizing reality with a positive feedback loop. His gift of time-consciousness surfaced.

"What time is it?" Director Oswalt yelled. "Let's centralize action; everyone focus on me." His voice had a commanding prominence, displaying a natural leadership, yet he himself was in shock. The experiment was succeeding beyond any expectation. The videos were recording all of it. He felt the urge to laugh and yell out loud, "Hey, we did it!" But first things first. Steve might be dead, or dying; there was time for jocularity later.

"What does Steve's EEG show? Is his brainwave activity normal? Is he experiencing the videos at the same rate we are?"

A technician yelled back, "Steve is breathing; all signs, including EEG, are normalized. We have brain activity, but, but…" the technician's voice sounded alarmed. Everyone started moving toward the technician's general location. As Oswalt was running to Steve's body, he looked at the videos. They showed a blank blue screen. He was overwhelmed. Had this really happened? Was this the end of the scan?

How had the video quit recording, only to end at that particular time of exactly 1 A.M.? His sense of timing was ringing alarms klaxons. Everyone in the room thought the same thing; this firsthand experience of being a voyeur to the past was extraordinary. There really had been psychic events!

Oswalt watched the technicians massaging Steve's body—he didn't look good. Steve was running a slight fever and began making low, moaning sounds. The technician looked at a screen, and then looked at Oswalt. "The only feeds that are coming in to the videos are from the coffin and Steve. We see no signs of tampering with the input! We still don't know how or what is producing the feeds from the coffin."

Oswalt nodded his head in acknowledgment. That was good news. The two feeds had stayed in stasis. Now, if he could only figure out where the red shooting beams were coming from.

Oswalt looked around at his entourage. "Does anyone here actually know or comprehend what happened? These events actually occurred, correct?" He said this, knowing there was nothing else he could do for Steve. Unless it was critical, or life endangering, he was going to continue. Oswalt owed that much to Steve, who had put all those years into this moment.

Oswalt listened and responded, knowing that he had to deal with one problem at a time. Too many more shocks and he would be ready for the asylum himself. "I need someone to verify where the feed is coming from. If we are being set up, I want to know!" As he said this, a shaft of red light shot out and penetrated the coffin, then faded out.

"What the hell is producing that?" Oswalt demanded. As he said this, he knew what they would find. Some psychic force beyond anyone's comprehension had staggered the mobility of everyone in the room. Oswalt saw everyone looking toward him for direction as he saw another beam of red light shoot out of the coffin. He felt cold chills go up his spine. "Is that damn light intermittent or regular?" Oswalt screeched.

Jed ran over to the coffin and started timing the light. Jed shouted to the Director. "The beams seem like some kind of precision code. It comes at ten seconds, then five, then ten, then three. It keeps rotating through that screwy algorithm. I don't gamble, but if I did I would bet this is some kind of code."

Jade spoke up first, addressing the most important point. "We have a true paranormal experience, sir. The first in over two hundred years!"

"Sir," a voice from another technician standing over Steve's body spoke. His voice sounding puzzled; Oswalt could see that the young engineer appeared to be in shock. "He seems to be calming down. His temperature is back to normal, and he seems peaceful. He has quit moaning."

Oswalt smiled a tight smile. Good news! Maybe the mission was attainable after all. Jade read the expression on his face and reestablished eye contact with him. "Sir, we can't make a100% identification, but the dresses, furniture, and accent all seem to match historical records."

"I agree," Oswalt said, slowly nodding his head while maintaining eye contact with Jade. He turned his attention back to the coffin and to Steve. "What the hell?" he said.

All eyes turned toward the coffin. It was still outlined in that reddish glow. There appeared to be a translucent reddish umbilical cord extending from the coffin into a spot midway up the wall. It also extended into Steve's brain. It was like a quantum tendril coming from the wall, into the coffin, ending up at Steve's brain. The red beams had stopped.

Jed and the other scientists were grabbing equipment and scrutinizing this latest event. It somehow just appeared, and it hadn't been there a second before.

"I am getting no power readings from it; it must be part of the quantum stream," said Jed.

Oswalt yelled, "Can you trace where that thing goes from the other side? Is it connected to anything else in the Institute?"

Jed hit his communication device. "Jones, is there anything happening?"

"No, sir," came the response. "All readings are normal."

"Double-check the power readings!"

"All power readings are normal, sir!"

They all felt the air pressure change at the same time. It was the same way that Bayou had explained his encounters with the psychic phenomenon.

The red stream had taken on a rhythmic resonance.

After the first time, the signals were understood. This meant the memory must be kicking back in; there must be some storage left on the scan that was downloading. Excited, Jade thought of this night wholeheartedly as her divine miracle. She glanced around and saw the surprised looks on everyone's faces. Either the videos were getting ready for more downloading or they were all experiencing a mass hallucination.

Was it her imagination, or was there a chill in the air? Jade's hair stood up and she whacked her leg to get moving. She ran back to sit in front of the videos. She knew as soon as she sat down that she would be a mental invalid to the video. It was a gamble, but in her brain it was an acceptable risk—and every historian's fantasy.

No one noticed the red umbilical cord turning a darker radioactive-colored red. The amplitudinously-designed wall of video recorders was flashing with a dazzling set of colors, which congealed into images.

Jade wondered how Steve was doing. The videos flashed and she was once again submerged, losing herself to the forming images on the screen.

Steve was frozen. He ceased counting the seconds. What was happening? He felt a concentration of exhilaration and fear. He didn't need an official diagnosis to understand that he was feeling delusional. He was no longer afraid of becoming Bayou. Steve felt that he could pull himself out. It was a good potentiality, he thought, not feeling confident at all. Steve was on one hell of a historical bender. He had questions. Was his soul leaking out with these exchanges? Was he now a quantum corpse himself? Had he been drawn into the many worlds continuum? Steve's academic reflexes still seemed to be working. He couldn't see or hear any information in this state, but he could feel it.

His brain probably wasn't doomed as much as it was being transformed. To what end and purpose, he knew; it was to resurrect the body of Bayou Savage.

Steve comforted himself with a silent prayer, which was highly unusual for him. "God, please don't let it affect me neurologically." Steve had been purposely tedious in experiment constructs. He knew that he was in one of three situations: first, and most likely, he was in a stasis coma in the lab, being fed Bayou's memory off the scan; second, the experiment had failed and he was now enveloped in Bayou's memory pattern, lost in the cosmology of the quantum world; or third, some other option he hadn't thought of, something he couldn't articulate. He was skeptical of any other possibility. Steve hoped, for his sake, that it was the first option. The other two options postulated a dismal future and he was too young to die. Wasn't he?

Steve speculated, wondering if the memory sharing had given him too much information to digest at once. His head ached from the slashing; he was having a hard time cumulating the data. He needed to do some mental grunt work. Steve was desperate and came up with a brainstorm that might help. He would ask himself questions that Bayou couldn't answer. If he couldn't answer them, then he knew that the Bayou template had completely submerged his ego, which scared him to death!

Steve ran down a list of possible questions, and finally came up with his favorite. He didn't dare ask any questions about music or paranormal ability, fearing that the Bayou personality would surface and completely take over—if it hadn't already. Einstein's famous $E=MC^2$. What did it mean? He listened to his brain and got no response, which gave him a tremendous feeling of relief. Bayou and that other voice—that narrator voice—hadn't tried to answer it, which meant that he still had some mental ego autonomy.

Steve began to slowly go over his conservation of mass equations. He then worked himself up to the E part of the equation, which he knew meant energy. He probed and listened, then tentatively went for the M's. The M's basically said that mass and energy were two forms of the same thing. Energy was liberated matter, and matter was energy waiting to happen. With mass, there were huge amounts of energy in every material thing. The squared part was the secret of the body—the guitar, the Bloodstone. The secret to unlocking the energy stored in matter was the ultimate secret to most physicists. Even the bombs that had been exploded two hundred years ago had only used a small part of their capacity.

Steve breathed a sigh of relief. He was still in here somewhere, despite all the slashing. His brain wasn't totally burnt. Now, if he could only survive the rest of the slashing till sunrise.

The history extrapolating was sobering. Bayou and Razor Savage were real people, not merely a legend. There really had been psychic paranormal events. The ramifications were staggering. Steve's brain was searching, as had Bayou's on the quantum connection of the guitar to the person. What was the activation trigger? He applied all of his logic and could not come to any believable conclusion. He wondered what Jade would think.

Jade, his favorite archivist was probably having a field day if the videos operated properly. He eschewed the guitar and its ghost-fighting abilities. He saw nothing that opened up the quantum properties that would put a body into a suspended animation. The guitar certainly had enough fuel to dissipate negative apparitions, but it was a reactive device. He knew that the guitar had the energy of thirty nuclear bombs—if he could harness the energy.

Steve remembered a late-night, alcohol-induced and seduced conversation with Jade. She loved late-twentieth and early-twenty-first century history. She told him that the two most commonly used guitars of that time period were Fender and the Gibson. Fender had the Telecaster, Stratocaster, and Esquire; to Steve the pictures all looked alike. The other model was the Gibson Les Paul, named after one of the earlier twentieth-century pioneers in the guitar Hall of Fame: Les Paul. Jade had gone on to say how she liked both sounds, and Steve laughed. They both had good old-fashioned sound.

Most musicians from that time period played loose, heavy stings with big pickups and overloaded Marshall tubes. Jade had played some music for him and got excited about the glorious fat, buzzy scream from the tube versus the transistor amps.

She had looked great that night, and they had danced for a while to some twentieth-century slow songs. That night he had no problems; the Institute was a million miles away, and he didn't want the night to end.

He had eloped with that memory quite a few times. Jade was beautiful and provocative, and exhausted every testosterone cell in his body. She had told him things she'd never told anyone else, all of the stuff that she kept to herself, all about her desire to travel back in time and crack the Bayou mystery. Jade also told Steve how she felt driven to understand Bayou's death. They had talked until the early sun cracked the dawn.

He smiled and began to stretch back toward the present moment. Better get back to business. He thought about the possible prognostications the guitar could have. It was obvious that the body and guitar were connected. It seemed, in retrospect, that the connection should have been discovered much earlier. But how did Bayou get the authority to engage the effects of the guitar, and what role did the guitar play in his ending up in the coffin? Steve didn't have the chance to finish that thought.

His brain skipped over the ending, and he felt the now-familiar memory slash beginning. The pain was blinding, but maybe he'd get some answers.

CHAPTER 10

❀

Bayou's voice came through the speakers, and the videos showed a hand picking up a twentieth-century guitar. Then they heard his inner dialogue manifest itself through the speakers.

"Man, it's hot; this guitar is the quintessential American power totem. Old, yellow paint, front and back pickup, pickup switch, volume, and tone control. It looks just like a regular guitar to me. The neck looked normal, except for the fret board, which looked pockmarked. Then, looking closer in between the frets at what appeared to be tiny pockmarks, I saw that those tiny pockmarks were actually very tiny crosses. The wood felt smooth. When Dad had cut it, he told me he hadn't intentionally set it up so these crosses would be in the fret board. The fret board side was already sanded and had a natural fret board shape.

"Dad looked at the guitar as I was holding it and said, 'The oak worked itself, and it really went fast. I cut the piece out and then cut out the slots for the frets, and put the machine heads on. I am 100% sure that whatever magic is at work comes from the fret board.

I rolled the guitar over and looked at the strap; she was plain leather, plain looks—nothing spectacular, your domestic, popular-version strap. I put it on and felt a chill settle down my spine.

Damn, I thought, *I hope this spooky Dark Shadows ghost-fighting ax works for me if what he is telling is true. But the last thing I need in my nomadic, quality-consulting lifestyle is to get hooked into enjoying this ghost-busting gig.*

Jade felt the immobility kick in. She wanted to attach a memory marker to look up the *Dark Shadows* reference, but her body was in slumber mode. She felt momentarily irritated. If she had the chance, she would have to crack this immobility code. *Some code, not force*, she thought, *has my body frozen*. She had studied psychology and was good at cracking computer codes. If she could find out more about Bayou, then she could crack this body code—if it was a code. She felt confused. She understood more about the twentieth century than anyone in the room, but she still felt overwhelmed by the memory feed. She didn't have time for any more thoughts. Bayou's voice began again.

"I thought a little about the quality of the guitar and the quality of my life. My life is pretty out-of-control these days, doing these quality gigs. The Total Quality Management revolution is pretty much spread out in too many different wavelengths and fusions. I stay confused, trying to keep up with it all. The main confusion is why businesses don't start quality programs, or they take the time and money to start a program and don't stick with it. The numbers are there. Everyone knows business results can be very sensitive to minor improvements in performance.

"For example, every year a study comes out that proves this point. This year it was the Institute of Directors (IOD), who reported in *Business Excellence* that a 1% boost in efficiency has a typical profit improvement of 1.9%, the equivalent of a 1% payroll reduction. However, quality programs that reduce costs or waste by 1% typically have a 7.9% increase in profits. Yet spending money to make money won't happen until there is enough pain. The days of cash surplus are a Corporate American fantasy.

"So with all the data on financials out there, how can a company not buy in? It's like this guitar; my brain is in denial about what it can do. Denial is also part of my quality life, just like the whole damn planet is about global warming. I have thought about my life, using my pretzel logic model, and here is what I know. Only a small percentage of companies ever truly achieve a world-class quality leadership position. Most of that small percentage of leaders failed to hold their leads, pointing to failures in leadership and governance. Universities have not been helpful in quality, leadership, or governance. It's classic blame storming.

Market conditions don't matter if you know your customers, business, and capacities. As it turns out, a company actually knowing this basic information is very rare."

Jade thought she would die: she was in historical archivist paradise. Thinking was not easy, but this was the real stuff. It was like she was seeing inside a resident of Atlantis. No one could counterfeit that speech unless they were from the twentieth century business world. She was exhilarated. The video continued.

"I thought with the end of the twentieth century and all of its excesses, our leaders would wake up—someone would see the light and there would be a rush toward the Malcolm Baldrige National Quality Award criteria. A great model asks the following questions: Do you have the right products? Do you have the right customers? Which systems do you have focus on? Implementing this program leads to measurable business results. Steve, looking through Bayou's eyes, saw Razor coming into focus.

"Razor had listened and finally spoke. 'Well, it's those Republicans' entire damn fault!'

"I ignored him and continued. 'Dad, it's pretty simple, and we'll discuss politics another time. Businesses monitor revenue; they monitor the cost of goods sold, and never ask how it affects the margins.'

"'Simple, right?' Dad said, and I laughed. 'Son, why, don't companies get this data?' Dad asked.

"'Ha!' I said. 'You'll never believe me when I tell you, because it's too incredible to be true. *Because it's free!* Companies can order the model from the Internet. Just type in Malcolm Baldrige National, download the information, get a competent consultant, get the top management to buy in; it's your tax and company dollars at work.

"'Instead, as I consulted these last few years and audited, I saw ISO 9000 compliance and the emergence of *Six Sigma*, lean manufacturing, and the *5 S* quality programs. Dad, my conclusion on this tangent—and I can tell that you think it's all the Republicans' fault—is that in the quagmire of quality implementation that has been my life the last few years, well, the leadership has failed. Greedership has succeeded!

"'A pretty dismal failure the corporate world was. There hasn't been a mandatory leadership buy-in at the top on the best quality/least cost—systems thinking. Mediocrity abounds, and the quality knowledge management systems' thinking and implementation always—I repeat always—get delegated! My point is that quality philosophy, like guitar playing, is simply systems understanding. Quality is a system understanding kind of gig. It pervades and cuts across leadership, ethics, and innovation. This is my famous Bayou Savage quote that has made me semi-famous in some quality circles.'"

"'Well, son, this is only part-time and none of that quality stuff you do will make a cornbread hell bit of difference until the Republicans are out of office.'

"'Okay, Dad. Like music, the syntax stays the same, but the semantics go through some ornamentation changes. I pretty much do everything that falls under the guise of Total Quality Management. To be honest, I love my job. It's different every day. Every day is definitely very, very different. In all my travels and all the kudzu thoughts that have filtered through my mind, Dad, this guitar has to be *the* trip. Dad, I feel a chill thinking about the guitar. I feel if I pick it up, my life will be severely and irrevocably altered.'

"Dad had that look, not one of compassion, generosity, or empathy, but one of his action-looks; his son, *it's-your-choice, you-decide* looks.

"'Okay, Dad, I can't wait!' I laughed as I lifted the guitar over my head."

There was silence for a moment, and Steve had time for one thought before the memory scan back on. Bayou, the man of mystery, was becoming more real to Steve. Listening to his outer and inner thoughts was almost too much to bear. His brain was soaking in the essence of Bayou.

Steve knew, with complete certainty that Bayou might never have picked up the guitar to fight ghosts had he not wanted his father's approval. He seemed tied up in trying to help the business world and didn't appear to have the time or desire to be a ghost–fighter. How had he been convinced? What was the catalyst?

Steve felt the memory slash rotation beginning, signaling another download.

"The phone woke me up at 4:10 A.M. My thoughts jumbled together. What damn time is it, and who would be calling me at this hour? Is Mist hurt or is it the college? Is it Stan, my stepfather, calling me about Mom's chemotherapy? Then I remembered that she was on her Canary Island trip. 'Hello,' I muttered, and thought, *this better be real good. If this phone call was from one of my former girlfriends, I will be very irritated.*

"'Bayou Savage?' asked the voice.

"'Yes,' I responded. I didn't recognize the voice on the other end. It could be one of my Total Quality Management clients, or maybe—maybe what?

"'Your father gave us your number, and kindly let us know that he is effectively retired. He also let us know that you are now his replacement.'

"'Huh?'" I said, sounding as confused as I felt. 'Dad retired from Dayco a few years ago, and no, I am not his replacement, so excuse me, good night.' I hung up the phone, wondering what that was all about. A few seconds later, the phone rang again. *Now* what? I was beginning to feel very irritated by this time.

"'You don't know me, Bayou, but please don't hang up. I was under the impression that all this had been worked out. I'm from the Institute, the psychic investigation group that your dad worked for. We have a hot one in your area, and we thought you would be the one to call. Your father told us, in no uncertain terms, to call you from now on, as he was retired. I believe he said the only investigating he was going to be doing was finding fishing holes.'

"*Yeah, sounds like Dad,* I thought. 'Okay,' I said. 'What do I do, where do I go, how do I need to dress, and whom do I meet?' Then it hit me—the most important question, the one I could not believe I had forgotten to ask. 'Do I get paid for this gig?' Even asleep, my scheming brain was looking for revenue. I heard a silence on the other end. Just when I was getting ready to hang up, I heard a long sigh, and then a frustrated response. 'No, you do not get paid, except for mileage and meals. It does not matter what you wear, but'—I heard what you might call a pregnant pause—'I hear that sometimes it pays to wear protective clothing against wood splinters and ectoplasm blasts.'

"'Say what?' I said. 'Run that last part past me again. What exactly do you mean, wood splinters and ectoplasm and protective clothing?' I had this sudden, bad thought. Has anyone been killed doing this? Thoughts were smoking through my head. First of all, how could I afford Kevlar vests and other protective clothing? My brain was hopelessly battered and still trying to wake up. I reflected for a moment. Had Dad mentioned any of this? If he had, I could not remember—and people dying, well, there are a lot of things that get my attention, and me dying is of particular interest, for some odd reason.

"'Well…' I heard on the other end, which reminded me of moments when I was doing quality audits of someone who knows the truth but is trying to be tactful. 'Well…' they said again. This person's little vocal habit was starting to annoy me. We have an adage in the quality auditing game that says, *Believe a confession, verify a claim,* and I just couldn't wait for this claim. I was sure this was a lackey, performing the bureaucratic end of things. I just knew that I was headed for a suicide trip. My luck—I was stuck with a minor Institute bureaucrat.

"'Was I ever wrong?'

"'Partner,' he said, in a voice that sounded like gravel and whiskey, 'I was out in the field doing this same job—same shit, just a different location. I can tell you, I got hurt quite a few times, but, luckily, there were no broken bones. No one I know has died. We have had quite a few suicides: people going insane, so to speak. I damn near did it myself. That's why I'm doing this white-collar gig. What you will find out, if you go into this, is that you have to be mentally tough to survive. You hear me?'

"I heard his voice and it sounded like he was freaking out. You have to be mentally strong! It's all unpublished, of course, but us liberators—he laughed when he said the word liberators—understand that our lives are on the line when we go out. I suggest that you not be too rash or too fast and that you take advantage of our checklist before heading out. That is, if you want to avoid a fiasco. Some of these spooks are bloodthirsty and merciless. They suck your brain like a mosquito sucking blood. Don't compromise safety; follow the principles in the training, and you will be fine.

"'What training are you talking about?' I heard myself say.

"'You haven't been trained at the Institute?' he asked in a low tone of quiet disgust. 'It figures. And of course your father, Razor, thinks it's natural. Just pick up the guitar and blow them away. Let me ask you a question. How strong and flexible is your brain? What phobias do you have?'

"'I'm only afraid of the dark,' I heard myself admit. I can't believe I told him that. Now it's my turn to be honest—excuse me, mentally strong—I don't quite see myself falling into that category. Mentally defective, mentally funny, mentally flexible, maybe, but not that marine-tough, *trim-your-beard-with-a-weed-eater* mentality that I thought my new friend was talking about here. Also, it seems to me that one certain father could have gone into a *tiny* bit more detail about the physical and mental demands of this job.

"'Tell me about the suicides,' I heard myself say. 'What exactly happened? Do you think it's a valid conclusion that it happened because of what occurred in the field? Also, please tell me about why you retired from the field. I am really curious, and I think it's important and—I might add—highly proactive to know. I have no death wish that I know of, and your last revelation kind of shocked me. I thought you were just the info-relay person and not a real, real...'

"'Field agent,' he said as he finished the sentence for me. 'Just call us field agents.'

"I didn't want to irritate him, but it seemed to me that the title 'psychic investigator' had a better, more distinguished, ring to it than 'liberator' or 'field agent.'

"'That's what I was for thirteen years.' He paused, and it sounded like he thought the number 13 was funny for some reason. 'No...probably just a coincidence; the years, though I have thought about it,' he continued. 'Thirteen years, an interesting part-time hobby, you might think. I was one of the best, besides your father, that is.' *Dad was considered to be good, that's good to hear*, I thought. 'But I always played it loose and dangerous. Too loose, and the last time, I must have wanted to kill myself. I went in way too cocky, with no preparation, and I am damn lucky to be alive. Of course I lost my hand. The damn ghost made me cut off my own hand, and then it laughed while I ran, screaming, out of the house.' He was quiet for a long time, lost in thought, probably remembering that encounter.

"He whispered, 'Tell your dad, Bayou, that I will be forever grateful. Razor heard about what happened and flew down, at his own expense, to terminate the ghost. That hot temper and damn miracle guitar of his—well, I heard he blew up the whole house; propelled ectoplasm for cosmic miles. It was incredible. After the battle, the only thing standing was your dad, surrounded by house debris that was spread out for thousands of yards.'

"'Then, when your dad came to visit me in the hospital, there were no lectures about being reckless, and no lectures about not being prepared. Instead, he told me to get my ass out of bed, get a new hand, and get back in the saddle.' He laughed, and I could hear my dad's voice in the background, playing the same speech I had heard a few times myself. Except mine was about what a waste it was to spend my whole adult life chasing women and playing rock and roll.

"He laughed again. 'Your dad's tough as nails, but he has a heart of gold. I never thanked him, never even asked about Lucille—the ghost that almost cost me my life and gave me the psychological bends—if you know what I mean. The thing I liked about your dad was that he did not brag. He reminded me of an extroverted Clint Eastwood, in a way. He got right to the point and did what had to be done. He didn't put up with bullshit and was always prepared. He hated bureaucrats and was extraordinarily self-reliant. You probably don't know this, but he had the best reputation of any of us. I'm glad he retired—got out ahead of the game.

"'One of my favorite memories is of your dad in a class about ghosts. He asked about his experience with his first ghost, which happened in North Carolina someplace. He wanted to know the nature of ghosts. He asked what would cause a good, Southern, flag-waving, Bible-thumping, trigger-happy Yankee-hater ghost to confuse him with a Yankee. We all burst out laughing—the instructor just rolled his eyes and let the class out early.

"'Bayou, this career—although usually part-time—has more burnout than any other occupation that I've ever heard of. Of course we have the art and science of psychic investigation down pat. All I know is that somebody—in my opinion, the Devil—drops the ghosts on top of us like rain, and we cowboys get to do the ghost tango with them. It's rare that we get a father-son combination. Usually we screen for situations like this. It could be very dangerous, if you don't possess the raw talents that your father has with the guitar. If you are a *stiff-minded brown-noser* and expect politics to get you somewhere here in the Institute, you won't pass the cut.

"'The only reason you're in is that Razor probably convinced someone that there is a needed genealogy to play the guitar, and that you possess it.' He sounded like he was enjoying giving me the guidelines. To be honest, I was intrigued. I sure didn't want to have my association with this group start off on the wrong foot. Damn sure if my life depended on their advice! He paused for a moment and then continued. 'The normal time for a field agent is six cases, or one year, then rotate or move on. A lot of the cases are bullshit, explained by ordinary scientific research. Usually someone comes in looking for excitement; someone pumped by one too many repeats of *Nightmare on Elm Street* or *I Know What You Did Last Summer*. Then, to compound the problem, one of our trainers told a glory ghost-busting story that they participated in, and it pumped people to think of the Institute as an extension of the *Ghostbusters* movie.

"'Your old man was one of the best, and I guess he wanted you to get involved because you're his son and you can play the guitar. Can you really play?'

"'Yes,' I smoothly segued. 'I put myself through college by playing bars, wedding receptions, and divorce parties: kind of the whole gamut of the relationship thing. I have the same capacity as Dad of being able to hear and play instantly what I hear. Whatever paid, I played. Whether country, rock, or top forty—just give me a crowded dance floor and an appreciative audience. I like festive, glow-in-the-dark Bohemian club music scenes versus the Grunge or Gothic overstuffed gloom-and-doom music downers. As I have grown older, I've enjoyed more autonomy in my music bands, being funded by my Quality gigs. And owning all the equipment gives you certain fascist rights. As for my playing ability, it all depends on the crowds. The band adjusts to the reaction of the crowd: good crowds get the premium gas; the urban banal downer crowds get the regular petrol.' I felt that I had impressed him with my years of service in the Bayou musical lifestyle fundamentals. 'Now,' I said, 'Where do I need to go to fight this ghost? And, by the way, what's your name?'

"'Quirk. My name is Quirk,' he said, in a rough-but-gentle finale.

The video faded for a second, then kicked back in. Oswalt had tried to look at his watch, but was unable to turn away from the screen. His question had to do with time. "How close to dawn are we?" Then he wondered if this was the reason for the acceleration of the video. What was the timeline? What was the objective? The Institute had been quite impressive back in their day.

Then Oswalt stopped; he was thinking about Quirk—the legend himself—and the most famous of all the Directors. Quirk had served and disappeared in the heat of the period before the big War. Oswalt forgot about Steve, forgot about Jade, forgot about everything except the mystery of what had happened to Quirk. History recorded that after Bayou "died," Quirk mysteriously disappeared. No one had ever figured it out. Police and Institute investigators had looked for a long time, according to Institute records.

CHAPTER 11

❀

Steve waited for the mental break. Instead, he felt himself being drawn in faster. He heard a voice, a familiar voice, say, "Quick, we are running out of time. Pay attention; your help will be needed later."

Jade and the other scientists all felt drawn in. Jade had time for one thought. "Steve, how was his body, his mind, and was that really the incredible legendary Quirk?" She smiled as she felt the mental suction reeling her back in. She also felt tears rolling down her face, and she didn't know why. Tears of happiness—maybe the years of fantasying—then all went blue and she fell into the memories.

"I had instructions from Quirk, and Dad had left me the official psychic investigator field agents' handbook—I call it the *Ghostbusters* handbook—to look through. I also had in my possession the latest memo on the logistics of being a field agent. I read it over as I packed my gear.

"I read the memo with great interest; it was totally different from anything I had expected. It also explained why Dad—according to Quirk—got so frustrated with the Institute.

❧

TO ALL AGENTS:

Optimization of Field Agent Brainpower, Confidential!

Point One: Recent validated research has provided some useful information. India has the lowest rate of Alzheimer's disease of any nation we know of; only 1% of the population develops Alzheimer's. The data indicates the use of curry spices, especially turmeric, which contains the antioxidant curcumin. Start eating more curry. **Point Two:** Fish oil is good for depression after a battle. Dutch researchers report that people with uni-poloar depression who added 2,000 milligrams of EPA-type fish oil cap-sules to regular medication halved depression scores in three weeks. Cause: Fish oil raises brain levels of serotonin, a mood-controlling neu-rotransmitter. Start taking fish oil capsules. **Point Three**: Folic Acid. To help keep memory sharp, start taking folic acid. Take supplements of 400 to 800 micrograms daily. **Point Four:** Take zinc. Helps recall words.

Point Five: Eat blueberries (or strawberries and spinach). Eating blueber-ries helps reverse the learning loss that comes with age. Eat one cup of blueberries or a large spinach salad daily.

"I bet Dad would have freaked, reading that memo! He would have consid-ered it obtuse and invasive, but he would have appreciated the information. He would have preferred some new information to use as a weapon, something to add to his psychic-fighting toolbox.

"Looking over the memo, I made a note to myself: eat more blueberry pan-cakes, find some Indian restaurants, buy some zinc and folic acid supplements. I usually take zinc when I have a cold, to augment the vitamin C I take daily. I use folic acid to help the occasional hangover, though I long ago forgot what the exact medical benefit was supposed to be. *Ha,* I thought, *better start with the regime as fast as possible with my brain.*

"With that thought, I jumped out of my car and headed to the location Quirk had given me. I figured that the drive out to the location would give me time to get up to par. *Just-in-time-education* you might call it. Thank God, someone had the foresight to include an audiocassette that had the quick and dirty *The Idiot's Guide to Psychic Events*, so to speak. I dropped the cassette in the car as I headed out to westbound I-40.

"The voice on the cassette started out, 'The following is a psychic overview,' and the voice sounded eerily like—I swear—the late, great Orson Welles. I started getting cold chills right off the bat, knowing that with this psychic group, it really might have been Orson Welles. Which reminded me that as soon as I found the time, I needed to acquire info fast about this group. The thought entered my mind that this might be some kind of *X-Files* conspiracy ring.

"The voice on the tape droned on with terminology that floored me. The tape went on for a very long time, all with references that made me feel exactly as if I were on the set of *The X-Files*. The terminology about apparitions and sensations when around psychic activity was overwhelming.

"I turned the tape off; my head and all my co-processors were working overtime. I could feel a sign flashing on and off in my head: Sensory Overload.

"I took the exit off I-40 that said 'White Oak,' going down a bumpy gravel road. According to the directions, there should be a house somewhere on my right. Sure enough, I saw the house on the right. It was painted a dingy white and had a sort of tombstone-like shape to it. It also had three—what did the tape call them again—'apparitions' standing outside. To be honest, I was scared to death. Here I was in the middle of Timbuktu, next to a big house with three ghosts standing outside, waiting for me.

"'Damn,' I muttered. These ghosts don't waste any time. One of the ghosts floated slowly over and said, 'Who the hell are you?' I smiled at how surreal this was, and figured out that it was probably a local redneck ghost, but then he reached over and physically opened the door. I didn't think that ghosts, redneck or not, could open a car door. I froze for a second, thinking that this ghost looked more like a real skinny true-life redneck.

"He grabbed my arm and said, 'Look, dipshit, what are you looking at? Are you drunk or stoned or something?' I knew something was wrong with my perception of the situation. Then I heard the redneck ghost behind him say, 'Just what we need. That damn haunt is on the jazz tonight, not letting any of us sleep, and we get a stoned idiot in our driveway. Send him home, Charlie.'

"It was then that I realized that these were real people who just happened to look like ghosts, due to the lights and darkness. I knew then that it was going to be a long night. I shouldn't have been listening to that tape; it had me spooked.

"'Quirk sent me,' I announced. 'I'm here to look at your spirit, or haunt, as you call it, with my guitar!'

"Ha, hoo, ho, ho!" They all three broke out laughing, falling over each other in their mirth. Every time they looked up they broke out laughing again.

"'Please,' the one called Charlie said, 'Say it again!'

"'Say what again?' I asked, perplexed.

"'Say what you just said,' he said, 'before, ya know!'

"'I'm Dr. Bayou Savage and I'm here to look at your spirit—of course with my guitar.' That was obviously not the right thing to say, because they all broke out into laughter again.

"This time Charlie said, 'What you going to do there, son, sing the damn thing a lullaby? Hee, hee!' And with that they all broke out laughing again.

"'First,' I said, 'I am a professional and the only hopes you have of getting rid of that ecto-...ectop...-well, that ghost, haunt, there, you have.'

"'Oh really,' Charlie said.

"I could feel my temper starting to kick in gear, when Charlie asked, 'How many cases you been on, Mister Doctor?'

"'Good question,' I answered. *Not enough to put up with this bullshit,* I thought to myself.

"'Now, if you will help me, let's get this equipment into the house and see how serious a problem you have. Is that okay with you?' I deliberately finished on a nice note. I figured it would be bad business to kick the ghost's ass, only to get my own ass kicked by real people when I was finished.

"We loaded up the equipment into the house, which of course looked and sounded absolutely normal.

"'Well,' Charlie said, 'she's waiting on you. Good luck. Don't get her too mad, because I don't want you to end up like that last guy!'

"'Say what?' I said, feeling a premonition that sent cold chills through my body. 'What other guy are we talking about? Not somebody from our organization, right? Right, Charlie? Charlie, talk to me.'

"Charlie looked away and smiled. 'You're different. No problem, kick some ass and we'll see you in a little bit. Ya know it's almost midnight, and that's when she really gets angry.'

"Sure enough, it was ten till midnight, and I started to get a little scared. Charlie looked at his watch and ran out of the house. I stood there, frozen, and wondered—not for the first time—what the hell I was doing there! First, I knew nothing about psychic phenomena. Second, and really more importantly, what happened to the other investigator? It was obvious that something really uncool had transpired, and Quirk had not mentioned it. That reminded me, it was dark in here; if I survived this encounter, I would break some other appendages that the ghost had not gotten to by wandering around in the dark. Then I realized that I was going to go through with it; I was my father's son. I always loved adventure, and here I was, getting front row seats to a hurricane-level psychic event.

"Five minutes had elapsed. I set up the video recorder and monitoring equipment, which included the environmental scanner. With one minute to spare, I hurriedly put on Dad's 53 Fender Esquire and turned on my little Fender Bullet amp with full distortion. *If I am going to die,* I thought in hyperdrive, *at least it's going to be with my kind of music: AC/DC, Def Leppard, old Savoy Brown, and Grand Funk.* Brain check: how did Grand Funk get their name? I've always loved trivia.

"Midnight. Nothing. Maybe my watch is wrong. I looked at the guitar. It felt good in my hands. The fret board was worn down from years of Dad playing it.

Fenders have their own feel; they are lighter than the Les Paul and tinnier in sound. They're great for country western, whereas Gibsons are great for rock. My latest axe, among axes, was my Parker P-38. Sweet guitar, where I practiced my Monte Montgomery licks.

"I have always had a special affection for a good Fender. I have played the Fender Strats, Telees, the old Mustangs, and Jaguars, but this Esquire was as good as they come. I played it a little bit, admiring the action, the newness of the strings. Dad had some ten-gauge on here, which made it a little tough on lead, unless I wanted to tune down to D.

"I decided that I was in good hands with this axe. It had a guitar gunslinger feel about it. I readjusted the strap, letting it hang low and enjoyed the feel. The guitar looked like it had a glow coming off the machine heads. I hadn't noticed it before and was curious about where the reflection was coming from.

"As I looked at it, I heard the first wisps of what I knew in the future would be the hallmark of Mike Tyson ghosts. The noise sounded like someone whispering my name in a three-dimensional chorus. Yes, it was my name—how did they know it? Out of nowhere, the wind kicked in.

"I heard Charlie's voice yelling outside. 'Hey, hoss, whatever you're going to do, do it now before it's too late!' Mayday! Mayday! My brain panicked. I stepped back to turn the amp on, and all the power in the house died. Not only did it quit, I felt something past my ear, barely missing my head. Now I was in total darkness and my brain was trying desperately to tell me something; my body was screaming *Get Out Now!*

"Don't think, do. The Yoda mantra was going max warp speed down my adrenaline corridors, and I was on the verge of doing some tactic—the smart tactic, I hoped.

"Where do I run? I froze. Fact is, if I run, I can't see. With my luck, I would kill myself—saving the ghost the hassle—and become the laughing stock of wherever these things come from. The next thought gave me a mental image of other investigators running, and I knew deep down that I was right to make my last stand right here.

"My eyes were tearing from the wind, and I noticed that the curtains beside my left hand were not moving. I stopped for a second, trying to figure that out, when I saw the ugliest damn green Aunt Esther—Sanford and Son ghost, about ten feet high, in front of me. The wind was picking up, and I knew it was going to be a quick ending unless I did something immediately.

"No power to my amp. I looked desperately for the tiny amp light. Can I play with no power? What song do I play? Damn Dad for getting me into this mess! It was too late for anything but action.

"I was freaking out! Pure panic kicked in, reminding me of one time when I almost drowned up near Sunburst, North Carolina. I felt that same panic: no air, no escape, and no way out.

"She looked at me and I heard a womanly voice in my mind. 'Welcome to Hell, Bayou; I've been waiting for you. Your third cosmic is going to taste so good, Bayou, Bayou.' The sound of my name was hurting my ears and the pressure on my head was killing me. My head felt like one of those chocolate cherries that someone had sucked the cherry out of. What the hell was a third cosmic? I knew I was in way over my head and flashed back to Dad's story about his Fines Creek Experience. What had he said? 'No electricity was needed,' or something like that?

"'Bayou, Bayouuuuuu…' I heard my name again, and my head experienced the worst crushing I have ever felt. It was like a voice that was boring straight through both eardrums! In total desperation I looked at the Esquire and played one of the oldest licks I knew. It was muscle memory and was my old, all-time favorite rock lick from Led Zeppelin's *Whole Lotta Love*, at the ending of the song after the chaos part. I screamed the notes in E and then, like a miracle, I could hear my guitar screaming with me.

"I reached down and turned up the volume with my pinky, the way I always did on stage. I didn't realize or care to remember that there was no way this could be happening. An electric guitar playing through an amp that was not hooked to a live power source does not play. I really, truly didn't care at that particular moment. All I knew was that I was going to die playing Led Zeppelin and I was going to play my heart out if this was my last moment on this planet.

"The guitar glowed nova and it felt like every string was on the verge of meltdown, but I didn't let up. I went right into the verse and heard the most perfect distortion in my life. The guitar then sent out a concentrated beam right into the ghost, and I felt an implosion that looked like a ten-foot strobe light exploding in my face. My last thought was, *I'm dead, Mist. I love you, sweetheart.* That, mercifully, is the last thing I remember before losing consciousness.

Steve felt his mind implode. "Hang on, damn you! Bayou, don't let me die here!" He screamed a silent mental scream, desperate to escape. He felt Bayou go out, and he didn't know if he had died or not. "Wake up Bayou, come on!" he screamed.

Jade and Oswalt felt the same thing and could do nothing but will Bayou to not be dead. She felt overloaded and knew she was losing her grip on reality. No one had prepared her, she dimly thought, and where the hell was Razor?

"Hey, wake up! Damn, boy, you still alive." I thought I heard Charlie's voice. I struggled to listen through the fog, and then I passed out again.

"Haywood County Regional Medical Center, room 207. Patient's name is Bayou Savage. Yes. Trauma, shock, bruises over 30% of his right torso and concussion, but yes, he's alive, Mr. Savage. No, he has not regained consciousness yet. He fades in and out and talks about Aunt Esther. Do you have an Aunt Esther you want to contact? What's so funny, Mr. Savage?"

"I heard Dad's voice coming from a deep bass amp, from some far-off place. It sounded like he was saying, 'Son, wake up and drink this; it's a holy water tonic from the Institute!' I felt someone tilting up my head and trying to drown me. 'Whaaattt??' I mumbled. I heard my voice in not only three dimensions—it seemed like a whole other universe. 'Whhhaattt,' I repeated, and then I felt like something like nitroglycerine flowing through me.

"'Well,' I heard Dad say to someone. 'Quirk, I believe he's going to pull through after all. That's my boy; I knew he had it in him!'

"'What's going on?' I mumbled. 'I just had the weirdest dream, Dad. You won't believe it, and you are going to laugh when I tell you.'

"'Car wreck; it must have been a car wreck to make me feel this bad," I muttered to myself. 'What happened to the car and how bad is the damage? It must have been one hell of a wreck!'

"I focused and almost saw Dad clearly. I heard concern in his voice. 'What car are you talking about, son?'

"'That car that ran over my head! What did I do, get involved in some kind of traffic jam? I don't remember how I got here. Is Mist okay? Please tell me she's all right!'

"'Here; sit up and drink this special drink I brought you. I think it might help.'

"'It's not white lightning, is it, Dad?' I managed to smile, but wasn't too sure about the stuff that he gave me.

"I managed a gulp and felt that power surge go through me. It felt great, really; I didn't know what the stuff was, but it had some kind of jolt to it. For some reason, it helped me focus better every second. I reached out for the glass and finished the remainder, then sat back in bed and smiled as I felt a healing sensation go through my body. I smiled again and heard laughter. I looked up and saw three bodies in the room. Two I recognized: my father and my daughter, who had just walked in. 'Hi, Dad. Are you all right? Wow, you look like you're glowing blue, or something weird is happening to your skin. Did they keep you down in x-ray too long?'

"I saw strange looks on both Dad and Mist's face, except that Dad was smiling, while Mist looked concerned.

"I saw that my skin was glowing blue, and a tingling was running from my throat through my whole body. Then the glow faded. I lay there totally out of it. Everything started to fade, and I heard the Mist say, 'He looks white as a ghost!' My final thought was that I had turned into a ghost-hunting smurf.

"'I had a dream,' I wanted to tell Dad and Mist. I remembered the ghost, but this was another dream. In this dream I looked out over my life and saw no successful relationships, no one to miss me if I had died. It was one of those dreams where you know that you are dreaming—not quite daydreaming, but close to it. I thought to myself, but I couldn't absolve myself of my moral responsibility and social circumstance. My only consolation was that at least I had a few mementos of love. Of course, the former spouses had more. Then I had a thought: Let's say that we are not really meant to be having long successful relationships as a species. *Maybe we are victims of a second-rate behavioral code.* If we were victims, then maybe the ghosts were victims who had to use their arsenal when threatened.

"Two weeks later, I had a feel for what happened. It was pure luck and primal instinct that saved my ass. From what I came to understand, later, the smartest move I made—and the one that saved my life—was playing the guitar and channeling the power from the guitar, through me, into the amp, which emanated an exorcisism sound wave that destroyed the ghost. The scanners picked up what those in the psychic world call an 8.2 on the earthquake epicenter. I had a copy of the printed scan results.

"The consensual opinion of the organization was that I had beginner's luck. Evidently, most people get fake reports and have to work a year or two before they hit pay dirt. *Lucky me*, I thought. I still harbored homicidal thoughts about Dad and the guitar. *Hey, guys, how about a little training before I go out next time?*

"I was okay, except for moving slowly and the occasional migraines, which I was told was absolutely normal after a heavy encounter.

"Of course Dad made it sound like it was a piece of cake. I asked him if he had any other sons, because it seemed to me that he was not overly concerned that I had almost bit the big one. It seemed to me that I had almost lost my life on a trip on the Ghost Disorient Express.

"I had to laugh, though. Dad was so proud of me, and it did feel good to hear him brag about the exploit. Most fathers brag on their son's hunting and fishing. I didn't like either. But this whole ghost-bragging thing he was doing was like going deer hunting your first time and shooting an eight-point buck. That is, if an eight-point buck was good; I sure didn't know.

"Dad sat down and smiled and we talked. We didn't talk about what could have happened, but instead focused on what I should have learned about the history of the organization, the equipment that I needed to work with and understand, and—most importantly—how the guitar worked.

"Two weeks later, dressed in jeans and shirt and just back from a business conference, I felt good. I told the people at my daytime job that I had been injured at a friend's house when their propane heater blew up. No one believed it, but it was the best excuse I could come up with on short notice. It had to be an excuse that worked and—more importantly—one that the insurance company would buy. The insurance and police investigators explained it that way, fortunately, and I didn't question it. I couldn't afford the hospital stay without the insurance money.

"So I spent every spare minute with Dad or on the Internet, getting updated on this whole psychic world. Research would help me avoid this situation again, if I could help it.

CHAPTER 12

Oswalt surfaced first. The videos had stopped recording.

"What time is it?"

He looked around. Everyone turned to hear the moaning. Steve was pouring sweat and looked like he was in bad shape. Jade stood, then toppled over. Embarrassed, she regained herself, not really caring what people thought. She had to get to Steve. The moaning was guttural, and he looked worse up close.

Jed and the other scientists were divided. She could tell they were torn between trying to care for Steve, monitoring the instruments and watching what the hell was happening with the coffin.

The coffin was now pulsating a dark red glow. The air had a distinct smell of burnt electrons and the tendril coming from the wall into the coffin had expanded into a yard-width across.

Jade knew that everything was accelerating. Her own head felt raw, and she knew it was coming to an end. She couldn't explain it, but sunrise couldn't be that far away.

Oswalt had a towel with cold water on Steve's forehead. Steve kept moaning and she wiped the spittle coming from his mouth.

Oswalt asked, "What time is it? My damn watch stopped."

Jed wished Oswalt would be quiet. He had noticed when they surfaced that all the clocks had stopped at four A.M. Sunrise would probably be in two hours if the four o'clock time was correct. Something was pegging all the instrument levels. Whatever it was, it was overloading the systems. Everything was redlined. How long would, or could, they hold up?

Jade reached down and whispered to Steve, "Please hold on, sweetheart." She yelled to Jed, "Can we disconnect him?"

Jed yelled back, "Go ahead and take off the attachments." Before she could react, the videos flashed and she felt immobilized. Jade, Oswalt and all the other scientists were helpless. The only mobility was in their eyes, which were all focused on the screens as they came to life.

Steve knew something was wrong. He felt weak and wondered how his body was doing. The grand finale was coming and he could feel it; he wanted to survive long enough to figure out what had really happened to Bayou. He gritted his mental teeth and he felt the slash begin again.

"Quirk called with a serious disturbance. 'Your assignment is a psychic disturbance located at a place called Woosley Heights, and it's in your neighborhood. One of our fellow investigation services had an experience there in 1973; it scared two of their best right off the mountain. Since then it has been abandoned and was finally bought. The new owner is scared out of his mind. The owner refuses to spend the night there. From what we can gather, at exactly one o'clock every night there is hell to pay for fifteen minutes. That's why we are assigning three of you; it sounds like a monster. We don't want you to be Tarzan on this, so we're sending you help. This one makes a bloody mess out of any pet in the house, and we think it's getting ready to go Mt. St. Helens, if you know what I mean.'

"'This monster ultimately kills any living animal host, from top to bottom, and creates all kinds of racket in fifteen minutes, giving it an enforcement code of 3, which means we send in 3 field agents to battle it. This prima donna ghost really amazes us. First of all, there is the noxious smell, which you will notice right away. It smells like something spoiled—fish or fruit or something. Then there are the exaltations, meaning it first does an audible broadcast. That is extremely rare! The message says that it is an ancient Magi, a primeval majesty. Then it goes on to say that it's a royal spiritual pontiff. And last of all, what makes this one different is that it knows that it is not part of this temporal world!' Quirk sounded distressed as he said this.

"'The Magi said that he was going to turn all the eggs into gold, due to his reverence for the creative principles symbolized. It happened just like the Magi said; all seven eggs in the refrigerator were found turned into solid gold.

"'Here was the Magi's quote: *I am turning the seven eggs in this domicile into gold. The eggs magically carry the germs of life over from one generation to the next, like Noah's Ark in the Bible. It is probably incomprehensible to your generational immoral finite mind, but you are the last generation. I am the harbinger of the new age; in exactly thirteen years you will witness the expansion and emer-*

gence of the creative deity evolving the mystery of cohesive chaos transformed into the one immaculate soul!'

"'We feel—and that includes me as well, Bayou—that you are in for one hell of a battle, any way you look at it. You know, this might be the real deal—this Magi. He might be the Pope, or president of ghosts.

"'The problem here is that this, well, this one kind of fell through the cracks. Thirteen years kind of snuck up on us,' said Quirk. 'We think the ghost impacted all worldwide psychic Institutes in some kind of stealth maneuver.'

"Quirk admitted, sounding a bit sheepish, 'We've just now completed the archive search on this. This ghost is philosophically and psychologically different; it has overridden the rules and is playing by a new set of rules. It's a whole new ball game!'

"'What about our fellow agencies?' I asked. 'Is there anyone else out there who can help, or do we even have equivalent agencies to work with?'

"'Not exactly,' said Quirk. 'Just networks fighting the same battle. Bayou, they are all frightened. This is not exactly a secret; everyone knows about it. I heard a rumor that a few of the other agencies have covertly sent people in, only to have them never return.

"'I can't substantiate the rumor,' Quirk continued, 'but nobody has responded to our SOS signal yet, except these two. The first guy's name is Bob Lace. He fought the ghost before and also has an enchanted guitar, much like yours. The second agent's name is Jon Ford. Jon is a new guy, who reportedly has some kind of a sonic psychic violin and is a friend of Bob's.'

"Quirk's voice rose slightly, and he sounded relieved to be giving me this particular piece of good news. 'Keep cool, Bayou; these two have been taking on ghosts nobody else would touch. Somehow, their wits, luck, studying, and comprehension of the materials—along with the combination of their talents—have allowed them to succeed with minor cuts and bruises where others have failed. Steve has even worked his violin with lightning bolts! They call themselves the *Desperados*, after the Antonio Banderas movie.

I laughed, despite of the seriousness of the situation. *Desperados* was truly a musician, guitar-playing-hero movie. 'Thanks,' I muttered. Time to call Dad and run this past him.

"On the fourth ring I got his answering machine, which always makes me smile. It is the shortest message that he could get away with: 'This is Razor. I'll call you back.' So the song, *On My Own, Again, Naturally* went humming through my head. I felt a cold premonition radiating from the back of my neck and throughout my whole body, like a nostalgic scary movie right before the big climactic scene. I don't like premonitions, especially spooky premonitions like this one.

"Arriving at the hotel, I immediately saw both of them waiting out by the entrance area. Bob was a tall, thin, lanky guy with black hair, around forty years old. Jon had long gray hair and looked kind of stocky around the midsection. Both had music cases with them. Jumping out, I ran over, introduced myself, made the official 'Welcome to North Carolina' noises, and loaded their stuff in the truck.

"'What kind of axe do you have, Bob?'" I noticed immediately that it wasn't a Fender case.

"He smiled and said, 'A 56 Les Paul with one pickup. Screams, though, on the highs. Jon makes his own instruments, including his violin.'

"As we packed up my car, *Boo*, I decided that time was passing way too fast. I had to get to know these guys, immediately. To kick-start the conversation, I asked Bob who his guitar idols are. This is one of the fastest ways musicians establish rapport with each other.

"'Eric Clapton and Joe Walsh,'" Bob said.

"'What about yours, Jon?' I asked.

"Bob jumped in and laughed again and I found myself liking Bob. 'I can tell you who he doesn't like for sure, and that is Charlie Daniels, who he thinks sucks, but everyone commercially loves.'

"Instead of answering, Jon asked me, 'Which are yours?'

"He smiled when I told him Roy Buchanan and Johnny Winter. I like Roy simply because he was a person who was truly complicated, a genius who self-destructed and no one could stop him. Johnny I like for staying with the blues. Papa John is my all-time favorite jam.

"We all felt the Magi premonitions then. The thought whispered urgently in my brain; this was not a trivial mission. We needed someone connected to the angelhood to fight this Magi, someone from the ashrams or Asian monasteries, maybe. I had always possessed a distinct disdain for dying, and here I was, surrounded by a false aristocracy of musicians about to meet—what do you call it? *Karma!*"

"'Diane Ackerman once said that music is the perfume of hearing, and that it probably arose as a religious act, to arouse groups of people,' Jon told them. Then he announced, "Boys, I made out my will before coming here. My ability is not psychic, but something tells me I'm not going to make it back from this one.'

"'This Magi is thirsty for blood. Its magic abilities and pure force out-power ours combined. The way I see it, this is a kamikaze mission.' As he spoke, he displayed the saddest smile I had ever seen.

"Then he said something that made both Bob and me laugh.

"'Since we're going to die anyway, let's blast into the place playing the music from Kubrick's *2001: A Space Odyssey*. That would, at the least, make our deaths dramatic enough for the CNN headlines!'

"We laughed. Bob turned around, and I thought he was going to spout something along the lines of, *if you believe it then it will happen*, traditional Pygmalion effect stuff, but again he surprised me. 'Bro, it's like this; don't go. Bayou and I can handle this. Go home, Jon.'

"The dreamy look once again reclaimed Jon's face. 'This one is the mother gig that I've dreamed about. The way I see it, we represent heaven, since we know that there is a God, there is the symbiotic relationship, and we have an advantage. See, playing for God, I'm not afraid to die. I'm not into suicide, either, though.'

"'Let's backtrack,' I said. 'It's the old saint-and-sinner paradox: Here we are sinners, yet we're representing God. Is that right?'

"'Yes,' Bob and Jon said in unison.

"'Maybe it's a question of context—or are we sacrificial lambs, like corporate executives when the firm goes down?' I asked.

"'No,' Jon said. 'I think it's that we have been so traumatized playing bars that we remain levelheaded in a crisis. We all have decades of bar therapy; we have the proclivity for being unflappable.'

"Bob asked a question. 'Exactly what do we have to inoculate ourselves against dying, and how do we go on the offensive?'

"I was starting to like Bob. Instead of harping on the death angle, he was in the *let's-get-on-with-it mode*. He wanted to know what we were facing and how we could best get a grip on it. There's nothing like planning your last set before you die to make you appreciate being alive.

CHAPTER 13

✿

"The house was a large contemporary, and when I saw it I vacillated between wanting to run away or walk away fast—I had narrowed it down to those two options. It was 11:30 P.M. and the night was clear, with just the right amount of humidity. We unloaded the equipment and waited for the owner to show up. Jon was still on edge, and Bob wanted to case the outside of the house.

"We all felt something in the air—a distant memory of something scary about to happen. I was doing fine till Jon said, 'Man, I've still got ghost hangover from our last gig.' As he said that he froze, I froze, and Bob—who had just come around the corner—froze.

"All three of our instrument cases began to glow with a phosphorous orange tinge. Simultaneously, we all smelled cordite and the cases were levitating about three inches off the ground! We all had the look of Pearl Jam looking at a Ticket Master distributor office.

"I heard Jon yell as I tried to think of the name for this psychic occurrence. 'It's started! It's the telekinetic force, and it's not even time yet! Boys, I am resolute, that is resolute to get my ass out of here! This is a primal force, not one of our pubescent naïve ghosts.'

"I agreed. I was certain that at this moment Jon and I had both probably thought of the need for fresh underwear.

"As I looked at my guitar, I heard Bob move around me. Then, in a tone of bewilderment and terror, I heard Bob whisper, 'Oh, no, no, no', as he looked up at the sky. 'Jon, it's a monition, and I'm pretty damn sure it's a prana!'

Above the house there appeared to be a wormhole of Biltmore-house-size proportions, and I heard the sound of a thousand bees humming through a

100-watt Marshall Amp at point-blank ground zero. Ted Nugent—like wailing noises came wafting through. I could feel time and space warping around us.

"'Bob!' I yelled, pulling together my last bit of John Wayne courage, 'What the hell is a prana?'

He yelled back over the wormhole noise, 'It's an energy that permeates the universe and usually manifests itself in a human form, supposedly tapping into the breath of the universe. Make sure you don't get possessed!'

"I had one of those stupid side thoughts I get on occasion that went something like this *this must be what a Marilyn Manson concert is like.* Then my adrenaline kick-started and I lunged toward the ole Esquire.

"Bob beat me to the draw and had his axe out. He said, 'Let's make a Custer stand inside the house!'

"I hesitated, then barked back, 'Why not out here at the wormhole?'

Bob screamed out something about the Plasmatics, revelatory cosmic entropy, and guitar inertia. None of it made any sense to me, of course, but he was the guy with the experience. Hmm. I had a miniature flashback; wasn't Wendy-O with the Plasmatics before she killed herself?

"I picked up my guitar and ran as fast as my six-foot, one-hundred-and-eighty-solid pounds under a max adrenaline rush would move me.

"We uncorked our energy reserves and ran into the house. The house now looked like a visual of ingested triple hits of acid with white lightning as a chaser. Lights flickered on and off, and my sense of balance was out of whack. My brain had no virtual reality reference. Thank God for the drugs I had done in the seventies! I had experienced and hexed out on a bad trip like this nightmare before. Of course I quit right after that, intending never to import those nightmare images again.

"I grabbed my axe, with no consideration of my amp, cords, or tuner—nothing went through my head, except that this was a psychic mach four hurricane and that I was in the Super Bowl of showdowns with virtually no experience. I did, however, stop to put on my ultraviolet head flashlight. One thing I don't like is surprises. I had read that some ghosts wielded pawnbrokered "Saturday Night Specials" that attacked agents with a force that could be seen coming—if you used an ultraviolet light.

I flicked on the ultraviolet light, seeing an impressionist mixture of brightly colored streams extending into infinity. I glanced at the other guys, who were adjacent to the living room sofa. They didn't have the UV flashes on, but mine was reflecting enough that we could see and hear the effects of what sounded like a Keith Moon solo.

"The ceiling fan above us started spinning at about 80 MPH. I thought there must be more than 220 volts shooting through it, and then I smiled; there was no electricity in the house right now except what was coming through the wormhole. All around us was the light glow of phosphorous, the cordite smell, and the twirls of brilliantly-colored light reflected from the UV head flashlight. I knew there was no hydroelectric plant in the world that could produce the power for these effects. Any rock band in existence would have sold their very own souls to duplicate these effects.

"That settled it. I didn't know about the other two, but I would need new undergarments first thing in the morning if I survived this. My courage was being replaced by a kind of Pink Floyd comfortably numb war fatigue, and the battle hadn't even begun.

"Like a cool scene from *Desperadoes,* the three of us grabbed our instruments in unison. Bob had that beautiful yellow 56 one-pickup Gibson Les Paul; Jon grabbed his homemade Stradivarius violin; I had my trusty yellow Fender Esquire. There was no time for smiles, strategy, or any of Covey's proactive life-effectiveness advice. From ghost punk to Tone Loc funk, the battle was going down, and I didn't have a clue what kind of music our Magi was into. This was our battle, and the ironic part was knowing how smart it is—no matter the extent of the emergency—to do the Covey 'pause and effect' versus 'cause and effect' plan; but now it was too late.

"This event had my whole lunatic attention. No time for contemplation, only time to die. My schedule with mortality was overdue anyway. My lifetime acreage had been over utilized; departure time imminent. I sent out a silent, but heartfelt message to my daughter. *Mist, I love you, sweetheart!* My thoughts were in full-blown panic, like a monumental cocaine overdose.

"We readied our instruments, and each hit out notes at the same time. This, in retrospect was really cool. We all hit E major at the same time. I was savoring that note, because this was something we had not talked about. E and A are about the fastest chords for guitar players to play, and E is the first one you usually learn growing up. E is the easiest chord to embalm an audience with.

"Consequently, I knew that Jon and Bob were playing some funky Hendrix/Parliament-sounding lick, staying in E but working variations and counter rhythms to attack the growing maelstrom. I always was exceptional at picking up and blending in, so I started a little AC/DC—ZZ Top portentous counter rhythm of my own. My eyes were on my axe, and I felt a tingling sensation over my entire body. I hoped I wouldn't break a string and was glad I had recently restrung with new Fender bullets. No matter what, I couldn't take my eyes off the lights or even look at the others.

"I didn't even stop to consider how I was able to hear the other two so well, with no monitors or amps. The glow and flow I had felt for years on stage before was now pure heaven. I also felt a coupling with their instruments of doing some serious guitar engineering.

"I heard yelling beside me and felt heat pulses in my hands. Bob was yelling something I couldn't hear, but his look indicated that I should pay attention to my axe—and something else. By now the turmoil was squatting over us like Lee Marvin in *The Dirty Dozen*.

"I knew, somehow, that we were in the center of all this bullshit, that all of the vehicles—and everything else outside—had been destroyed. I knew Waynesville had just lost its virginity to spiritual invasions. I knew that my comprehension of this situation was inferior, and that this encounter might be the extinction of mankind if we lost.

"Bob had this engrossed look on his face. I knew that he was trying to tell me something, something critical. But I had no way of hearing him over the deafening ear quake that had become married to us.

"I felt those heat pulses again in my hands, and thought I was losing my mind. What I was seeing was impossible. I looked at my guitar and did a double take. The frets on my guitar were melting. Now the ghost had my undivided attention.

"*If I survive this damn ghost*, I thought, *this guitar is going into the Institute's Hall of Fame. I just hope someone remembers me.* I kept playing, feeling the strings cutting into my fingers. I composed my thoughts and wondered what the metal frets in my guitar were made of. I snarled and was pissed that I hadn't paid more attention to that during my musician travels. Maybe I could have used diamond frets or something, instead of getting my ass kicked in this citadel of a homicidal magi. I felt a panicked laugh bubble up, and knew that I was suffering under the ghost's environmental constrictions.

"Somewhere, in the back of my mind, I considered other leads to play. I did a video virtual scan, but couldn't pull one out. As I played, I felt no pain and didn't notice any searing or burning sensations. More than anything else, this must have been how David felt when facing his Goliath.

"Just as my confidence was growing, I heard a boom, and a significant sonic concussion knocked me against the wall. I was banged up but the guitar was still intact.

"I glanced over at Bob and saw that Jon was not with us. We both looked around, and I heard Bob cry, 'Noooooooo!' I knew that this was no illusion. We were up shit creek with no paddles.

"Jon was silhouetted against a black background, alone, playing some kind of jam that made white lightning shoot off his bow against this large, monstrous, descending black shadow. As I watched and Bob screamed, the shadow—which looked like a multitude of merged shadows—had completely engulfed him.

"Jon's violin playing was shrinking in volume. Then we heard a hell-splitting high note. The note had the intransigence of one who was giving up his life to hit that note. The note was the ultimate, arrogant life-note—the ultimate power note.

"'Hold on, man, I'm coming!' Bob screamed again. He floated up, with his axe, levitating, and began to play at full psychic volume. Just as he started maxing his volume—and I regained my senses long enough to start playing—the sound we were waiting for came through. The Michael Jordan of guitar licks erupted from our guitars. The shadow imploded into an orange-black ball of levitating flames, about one foot in diameter. We saw the faintest flick of Jon's shadow, and then he was gone. All the commotion seemed to freeze in that moment.

"'Jon, no!' I heard Bob yell. Pointing his Les Paul at the remnants of the orange ball, Bob screamed out, 'Die you motherfucker!' and flew, with his axe, directly into the flame. I watched, mesmerized, as the yellow glow of Bob's axe merged with the orange-black flame. His guitar made a symbolic yellow rocket of ectoplasm, shooting straight into Jon's adversary.

"Bob was completely insane now; he looked like a crazed Springsteen in concert, or Meatloaf on speed or something. Whatever it was, I could feel the power of his axe and knew he was in a death-lick dueling spiral. He was going to blow all the psychic power that emanated from the guitar and him.

I reacted without thinking and propelled myself toward Bob. I raised right off the ground, completely oblivious to any fear or surprise that I should be flying. I felt storm-like static all over me.

"I joined in with Bob's aura, but only on the outskirts. His death keel separated him from me; I had never experienced the energy off my own axe that I felt from his.

"Bob was still screaming—not that I could see him—but I could more or less feel what was happening. I intuitively knew that I had to commit everything now, or it was over. We hadn't even seen this Magi, and we were being decimated. Damn! I hoped this wasn't his opening act.

"Bob was committing suicide in front of me, and somehow we were fighting this ghost with our guitars, floating ten feet off the ground. Then I saw it. The Magi stepped through the portal. I could feel myself being dwarfed by its power. I listened for any conversation, any opportunity to help Bob. Bob had seen the figure step through the portal, too, and aggressively jabbed his guitar toward the Magi.

"The Magi turned to look at Bob. With a single look, powers shot out from him. I couldn't tell where he had shot the powers from, but I knew it somehow radiated from the Magi. As I went to match power-for-power, my life flashed through my mind. I have always been an amateur. Briefly, I considered my family.

"I screamed out my daughter's name and poured every ounce of soul power into *Highway to Hell* by AC/DC. Everything crescendoed. Somehow, the house had vanished. I got a close-up look at the Magi: it had an anvil head, black eyes, and looked truly evil.

"'Well, Magi, it's time. Die-ga!' Bob yelled. I heard and felt Bob going nova. I tried to match my own energy with Bob's, but it was like a matchstick next to a bonfire. Bob was pouring out all of the grief of losing Jon. A teardrop glistened its way into each deadly lick. I couldn't hear the music, but I knew he was kicking in some deadly Van Halen—Stevie Ray Vaughn speed licks, as well as picking up other world-blowout vibes. He intuitively knew what to do—or let our axes pick the way—to send this monstrous, anvil-headed creature back to where-ever-the-hell it came from. His grief and energy were overcoming the ghost.

"My fingers were now a blur on the guitar neck and I felt myself merging with Bob. Not just Bob's aura, but actually merging with Bob himself. I experienced a rush of emotional grief that made my own tears flood, but I kept playing. Then, all a sudden Bob and I were one, playing the same lick with the same heartbeat. I felt better than I had ever felt in my life. I heard heaven, I heard voices in twenty-part harmonies, and I saw dimensional doorways opening and closing around me. I knew that we were no longer in the house; we were in the eye, attacking the source.

"I could feel the evil; a vile brackish odor tainted the back of my throat. I let Bob take the lead, let him guide our joined leads. I screamed, 'Die, Die, Die, Die,' as I looked directly into the Magi. I felt the battle turning our way. I heard a group of demons howling and gibbering. I heard languages—dialects in three-four-and five-dimensional warps. My own protoplasm felt like it was being blasted apart. I kept my fingers glued to the keyboard, knowing the instant I stopped my life was forfeit.

"The odds of surviving this encounter were not good. I had made it through countless close calls, but never had I faced a primordial deity. The consequences to my body, if I did survive, were not even worth thinking about. The heat was prevailing, and the sweet personal relationship with my guitar—the feel, the response—was slipping. My mind was suffocating. Bob and I were a unifying element fighting for the forces of good.

"I saw it before I felt it. Bob's aura lessened, and then he let out a death scream. It sounded identical to Jon before he died. Bob fought back, but the Magi's power seemed to be directly focused on him. The Magi was yelling in some unintelligible language as orange pyramids blasted out of his hands, destroying the last of Bob's defenses.

"I felt Bob die. It was as if he was there, then gone in a nanosecond; the song remained the same, but he was gone. His unique Les Paul sound was extinguished. Briefly, the pyramids flowing out of the Magi's hands started circling me—some looked Incan, some Egyptian. A tyrannical headache attacked me that I knew Bob must have felt before he got blasted. My supernatural Fender was glowing bright green now. The conflicting colors of yellow and green made a parade of chaos. The machine heads were breeding a fireworks show worthy of any Fourth of July display I had ever seen. There was no time to grieve for Bob and Jon. The only thing I felt was Bob and Jon's last note reverberating through my soul. They had both died in A minor.

"Vapors of brimstone preceded the Magi as it moved closer to me, smelling of death. I smiled to myself and hummed a little Roger Miller jingle I used to sing when I was a kid: 'Knuckle down, buckle down, do it, do it, do it.' Then I experienced a sudden, but welcome, inspiration.

"Jon fought the Magi on the ground level when it had separated him and devoured him. Bob fought it head-to-head and lost. I could either sink low and come up from under it, or try another approach. I knew the secret was to let the force pass through me, then attack.

"With this rationalization, I decided to slow down—versus speed up—and hit the opening blues licks to Three Dog Night's "*Momma Told Me Not to Come.* All space and time had melted by this point, but I laughed again. I knew that this demon was trying to use time and size distortion against me.

"I survived my drug days—I was going to dig deep and kick its demon ass with some sweet licks off this ole axe. I never really could distinguish the opening lick I was playing from *Born on the Bayou* by CCR. They both sounded the same: hotter than hell and priceless to me at this moment. Using this strategy, I hoped to throw off the Magi's rhythm.

"The pyramids and ultraviolet-light attacks turned from yellow to pink to red. I felt a lessening of the attack, but it wasn't enough. I knew that I was going to die, but at least I had tried to save humanity. I'd go out as a hero, not a spectator—a doer who had, as Garth Brooks said, 'stood inside the fire and poured all of my essence, good and bad into this battle.'

"After the opening licks, the Magi paused. A nominal silence, which gave me hope as a vigorous development for the good guys. Make that good guy. I kept forgetting I was the last one left.

"I wished Dr. Strange, Dr. Fate, the Phantom Stranger, the Specter—any of my old testosterone-loaded comic-book heroes—would show up. *Please,* I silently prayed, *if any of you guys are based on real-life events, now is the time to show up! Just whisper some easy-to-follow survival tips in my ear, please!* How about Dr. Dre, Tupac, or Public Enemy showing up? I thought, as my body burned through hundreds of *I'm-Going-to-Die* calories. My fingers were dying. I was dying.

"I *was* dying. I felt it; the pressure in my head was killing me. My body was giving out, and my strength was used up. I needed some rest, just for a second. Tears were flowing out unchecked. I didn't want to die. Pure panic was fading in my body as my mind tried for one last effort. I felt my desperation seeping away. I had no last-minute intelligence. I was too tired. I felt the guitar slip out of my hands.

"*Something was happening.* I felt my strength waning, but the guitar began to glow and grow hot. I couldn't figure it out. For some reason, I couldn't focus. My fingers were bleeding, and the guitar began to shoot sparks into the enfolding darkness.

"Then the guitar was grabbed out of my hands. Blind and helpless, I heard that sweet riff, and tears sprang to my eyes. It was my dad's playing. Dying, blind—my last experience would be a good one. *Thank you, Jesus.*

"I cried and listened to the sounds of my childhood, the licks of my earliest memories. Dad was playing hard and fast, and his aura was pulsating bright green and blue. I didn't know how he'd gotten here, or where he had come from, but he was there—we were together. I wasn't going to die alone. I tried to focus, wanting to make sure that I wasn't hallucinating. Although I felt his body beside me, I still wasn't sure he was actually there.

"*Dad, I love you*, was my final thought before oblivion struck me between the eyes. I heard *I am a Pilgrim* played at Van Halen speeds in my subconscious as I went under. I died with a smile on my face, remembering being a kid, sleeping under the piano beside the beer cans, listening to Dad play that song. It was one of my best memories.

The video paused for a moment. Everyone looked at each other. The room had a red glow everywhere you looked. No one had a dry eye. No one had time to react before the video brought the room back to the focal point.

Oswalt felt that Bayou was trying to force-feed this information to those present to help them understand the next step, which meant that there was some kind of plan afoot. He wished that the Institute had the body-repair holy elixir recipe.

Jade couldn't get her brain together under the deluge of emotional weathering. She was starting to understand Bayou and what he was capable of—his strengths and his failings. The person behind the legend was more incredible than anyone had ever imagined. She wondered if Steve, positioned at ground zero of this memory deluge, could possibly survive the onslaught. It felt like a jet of fire-hydrant water blasting through a straw. The extreme pathos was overwhelming.

Steve heard a voice talking to him. His physical body was pouring tears; his mind, though, was reassured by the voice. "Steve, snap out if. This has already happened a long time ago. It's history. I need you to understand that so we can thaw the body when this is over. Do you understand?"

"Yes," he mentally responded.

"We don't have much time. Hang on. We still have more to go. You need to understand the Bloodstone, because it will be our way out of this. Pay attention. I need you!" The voice faded into images.

CHAPTER 14

❀

"'Try to remember,' I mumbled to myself. What happened? Was it a motorcycle accident? Did a wild statistician attack me in a seminar? Maybe I was playing a bar and tried to break up a fight. No, none of those rang a bell, and who was that guy next to my bed?

"I had surfaced in a hospital with dad in a coma next to me. The first image to greet me was a tear-stained Mist, smiling. It was good to see her. She was trying to tell me something, but I was having a hard time hearing her, for some reason.

"Mist also knew that Razor got me into this deal. She loved him and feared him, like we all do. Now he was in a coma. It was funny in a way, because we always thought he was invincible. Even though she didn't show it, I could tell that this was affecting her.

"It took time for the realization that some thirty-three other agents had died in battle. Only Dad, a 19-year old girl, and I had survived. Quirk said the girl made it only because of some mystic Bloodstone from ancient times. She used this stone the way I use my guitar.

"The question remained: How did Dad penetrate the battle zone? It had to be the link with the guitar, and I was using it when he approached.

"Quirk said he didn't know, but that the girl came out of nowhere. No one knew who she was, and maybe this Bloodstone helped Razor do what he did.

"I found it refreshing that everyone was curious, but no one was willing to challenge Dad's survival. His reputation was larger than life, and his integrity, as long as there are no women involved, was never in question.

"Dad's theory was that high-maintenance things pirate you of your energy. He had a hard time with the concept of codependency, for example. He thought that if you were that weak, then you deserved it.

"Quirk informed me that civilization was still alive and well, due to the sacrifices of the field agents. It was like World War II D-day for all psychic investors—and we won. The cost of casualties made it look like we won the battle, but—and this was the true question—had we lost the war?

"We needed more data, and no one had ever seen an event like this. Dad and I had become minor celebrities in the paranormal world. We refused interviews out of respect for Jon, Bob, and all the other sacrificed agents. I was hidden away at the Institute's Retreat. Dad was at his house, working on cutting the grass and conducting business as usual.

"Quirk and Dad stopped by the Institute a few weeks later to give me an update. Quirk, as usual, went straight to business.

"'Only one thing could be agreed upon; there was a sequential consecutive series of events in Waynesville, North Carolina, that had unleashed a primal force that left mortal, serious, and collateral damage.

"Quirk said they remade the guitar, Dad jumped in, or tried to get the guitar rebuilt, and it played well, but I don't know…I don't get the same vibes as I usually do when I pick it up. But I would like to see if that Bloodstone that girl has might act like a catalyst to activate whatever it is that activates it. What do you think?

"Quirk quickly responded on the defensive and said, 'Our mission is to bust ghosts and put to rest tortured souls and restless spirits and expose the frauds. Our vision is to be in business as long as the previous factors exist. How we make it happen is by trying to survive and stay one step ahead of the competition for private sector grants.'

"'What about this girl and this Bloodstone she has? When can I meet her and what have you found out so far?'

"'Interesting case, that one; she's an enigma. Her name is Leslie Quinn. I know that she's young, and through some miracle she was saved from certain death at the battle. The only three survivors found were you three!'

"Quirk paused. 'I also think, Bayou, that she somehow saved you and your dad's sweet asses. That's about all I know.'

"He continued, as if reading from a script.

"'She first came to our attention when she was ten. She's from King's Mountain, North Carolina. She attended some private rich-kids' school in Charlotte, and according to our reports, was normal until things came to a head in the fifth grade.

"'She had a habit of talking about her connection to the ancient Druids. She would give great elaborate stories of how her family ancestry went way back. All of her school classmates and teachers reported it, but it seemed like a harmless childhood fantasy.

"'What happened next—and what brought her to our attention—is that her class went to the King Tut traveling exhibit down in Charlotte. That's where it gets interesting. When this little girl saw the exhibit of a mysterious stone called the Bloodstone, believed to part of some mummy/religious ritual, she froze and would not move.

"According to eyewitnesses, she went up to the display case, mumbled some words, and went into a trance—and then the impossible happened. Bayou, keep in mind, this was all recorded by the top-notch museum security-camera system.

"'The stone began to levitate, passed through the glass unbroken, and landed in her hands. Then—and this is the best part—she and the stone both disappeared. Totally disappeared!

"'The part that intrigued the Institute was what happened when the school personnel called the parents. Pay attention—this is the best part.

"'They called her parents to apologize for misplacing their daughter. As they tried to explain what happened, the parents interrupted them and said not to worry. It was normal for their daughter to pull stunts like this.

"'The parents apologized and said—get this—not to worry, that she disappears into another dimension and is usually back within three hours. It was perfectly normal for her to do this.

"'The parents also said that she would teleport herself back home, as was her habit.

"'When she appeared out of nowhere in their living room, the police, State Bureau of Investigation, and school officials were all waiting. She appeared in the blink of an eye in the living room, completely surrounded, with a smile on her face.

"'From what I heard, the police about crapped in their pants. The opinion was that the parents were professional magicians and this was some kind of prank. Their investigation pulled up nothing that would indicate any information along those lines to substantiate that line of investigation.

"'When the museum officials asked for the Bloodstone, the girl announced, matter-of-factly, that it was time for her to possess it. She said that the axis was now aligned for her to take possession.

"'We believe, from what we can piece together, that she already had teleportation and transdimensional power before the stone. We believe that she and the stone have some designs on future events, and we don't know what the stone is capable of.

"Quirk said, 'What she pulled off at Woosley Heights had to be at least the equivalent power of 33 of the world's best psychic agents' talents.'

"'I'm curious,' I said. 'What has she been doing since the age of ten? That's a long period of time for someone with those powers.'

"'During our interviews with her, she said that she was practicing. When we asked her what she was practicing for, she said the *Magi Event*. At the time, of course, we didn't know anything about this supposed event, because the Magi affected our records and memories.

"'After the event, we looked at her records. She knew it was coming, Bayou. What part she played, we still don't know. She was pretty banged up, too. Her parents asked everyone to leave them alone to give her a chance to heal. All three of you have been depositioned, and I'm waiting for her to respond.

CHAPTER 15

❁

"A note arrived as I was talking to Quirk, from no one other than Leslie. She wanted to meet me. When I arrived at her house, the smell hit me first. It smelled like some kind of incense. Sweet, yet not overpowering. The posters on her door looked like the typical teenage anarchy. The music sounded like ole Fleetwood Mac playing.

"That made me smile; anyone who liked Fleetwood Mac had at least a modicum of good taste. The door opened to a girl about five feet, six inches tall, around one hundred and forty pounds. Her back was turned toward me.

"'Hi Bayou,' she said, without looking back.

"'Remember?' Leslie asked me. 'I pulled yours and your dad's asses out of the fire back there in Woosley Heights. She kept on going, and no, I thought to myself, I didn't remember that! But I kept listening, storing that info away for a later time.

"'By the way, your dad and daughter are a piece of work! I'm worried about his diabetes, though; he'll only have his eyesight for a short time before it kicks in! Your daughter is thriving and giving life a marathon workout!'

"As I waited, Leslie changed the subject strictly to Dad.

"'He really worked a miracle!' She continued, 'He—and for that matter, you—have very little *real* power; the guitar is cute, but it's limited. As I was approaching the house, I had been watching the channel you were on. When you went down, your dad picked up the guitar and pulled out a 60% power boost from the Bloodstone. No one has ever—I repeat, ever—been able to access the Bloodstone in over 2,000 years, besides myself. Somehow, he reached out and found the Bloodstone and drew upon its power, integrating it into the guitar.

"'I haven't contacted him yet to ask him how he did it, but if I had to guess, it would be that he used the guitar as his amplifier. When his power started to fail, he searched with his remaining strength and connected and basically took over the Bloodstone. I was going to fight the Magi, but your dad took over the Bloodstone, and I threw in with him, following his lead.' She shook her head with an air of disbelief. What did this girl look like?

"She continued. 'I was looking forward to this encounter, especially meeting the famous Bayou, and I can't wait to meet your dad!' Still looking away, Leslie continued in a voice that was light but with a slightly sweet, sarcastic tone. 'I was tied up on Magi strategies and didn't get around to it until too late. I guessed, in the aftermath, that I would have been dead like the other agents if it hadn't been for Jon, Bob, you, and your dad.

"'But when you went down, I freaked out. I was focusing on defending myself and trying to find an offense when your dad showed up. I couldn't protect Jon, Bob, or any of the other agents. The Magi was too powerful.

"'Then your dad put on a hell of a monster show with that guitar. It sounded like damn Lenny Kravitz at his best. You put on a pretty good show yourself; I registered about a 20% power surge from you there at the end—not bad for a rookie.'

"Was she ever going to talk to me face to face?

"'I had been put in my place by this 19-year-old pro who seemed to be displaying *synaesthesia*. Synaesthesia is a clear mental impression induced by the *incense*—I was guessing here—to read my *channel*, including who I was, why I was there, my father, the whole nine yards, before I ever opened my mouth.

"Common shamanic practice, I read once, does not rely strictly on drugs or incense, but drumming. I laughed to myself; I bet her powers have nothing to do with the incense or the drumming from Fleetwood Mac. She probably likes those things; her real power comes from that Bloodstone.

"Leslie turned around to look at me and smiled. She was beautiful, with blond hair down to her shoulders, a kind of intelligent, roundish face, with perfect alabaster teeth. Her blue eyes flashed with mirth as she gave me a brewed-up, mysterious look.

"It was almost as if she could read my thoughts. She said, 'So, you like the incense and music?'

"'Yes,' I said, smiling back, drawn by her charisma. 'I'm here to invite you to join the Institute. More important to me, though, is can you help me put the power back into my guitar?'

"'Sure,' Leslie said, and reached around to pick up the most beautiful stone I had ever seen. It looked like a piece of bright red amber. It was about as big as my hand and transparent, with that blood-red hue. Then I realized that it really was a piece of amber.

"'How amazing,' I said in my most eloquent voice. 'It really is a piece of amber. How does it work?'

"'It's simple,' Leslie said, and smiled.

"'Excuse me,' I said. 'Could you break down *simple* for this *over-the-hill* myopic mind, please?'

"She had that young, natural smile that I concluded could be an incredible incentive to the all the young nature lovers out there.

"'To begin with,' Leslie said, 'most people use only about 5% of their brain. I use about 15%—okay, maybe 17% of mine. All the shrinks have told me that I might secretly be the start of the next human evolution, Human Superior Sapient. I personally think that it doesn't matter.'

"'My IQ does not really help me out; it's been tested at 130, so don't think I am a super genius or anything. There is something in my brain that triggers perceptive experiences and abilities that the normal human brain is potentially incapable of. But, well,' she stammered, I have *additional* senses.

"'I don't usually explain it to people…' Leslie paused and looked down. 'I can go into a mental no-man's land. I feel precognitions—I have visions, waking dreams, see the future, and get in touch with the multiverse. I like to think my mind is the computer that accesses the supernatural Internet.

"'The Bloodstone boosts me up to 5 gig Mega-hertz Pentium processing speed.'

"'That would explain how you survived,' I said, "when thirty-three other people died. By the way, thank you for saving our lives. My father and I are grateful for your help.'

"'Actually,' Leslie said, 'between all of us, we provided just enough of a distraction to allow us to surprise the Magi. I don't think I could have done it alone.'

"I understood then that this girl had power. If she wasn't bluffing, and I knew she wasn't, she had incredible powers."

The video faded to black. Jade finally grasped a breath of fresh air. Everyone reached for their heads simultaneously. They all felt the pressure in the room lessen. The room was still surrounded by the red glow emanating from the coffin. Oswalt looked at his watch; it was now five A.M. What was he supposed to do? His head ached, but one thought overrode the others: what had happened to the Bloodstone?

One of the scientists yelled. Everyone looked over at Steve's body. He had blood coming out of his mouth and one ear, and tears streaming from his eyes. Submerged deep into the memory, Steve felt pain through and through. He knew that his body must look like hell. Whatever opinion he had of Bayou was forever changed. Hell, he had *become* Bayou. He felt the paternal misgivings of parenting Mist, the loss of his mother, the connection to the guitar—all of it. It was the most bittersweet moment of his life.

Everyone in the room sensed that the end was approaching, as they felt the pressure building. Was it time for the grand finale? Then they were submerged into the primal angst one more time.

The videos came back on and Leslie's voice started.

"'And Bayou, you will be happy. As I see it, extraordinarily happy. The divine intervention will be a force of good, not evil. I feel this. It will happen when you are thirsty, in a dark place, a nightmarish place that you will be praying to escape from, and then it will happen to you.'

"With that last word, she shuddered and appeared to be waking from a dream state.

"'Leslie,' I asked, 'are you all right?'

"Leslie looked up, took a deep breath, and regained her composure. 'You have to wait for the time, don't you understand? Some things we can change; some things we cannot.'

"Leslie smiled that beguiling smile again. 'I remember you thinking that if you ever met me, you would challenge my history, given the chance.' With her smile still in place, she changed the subject.

"'Bayou, go take care of your father and daughter. You have three weeks before Quirk will call to tell you of the next big danger. I should have your guitar hexed, backed up, and ready to go by then—and I predict that you will need it!

"With that Leslie smiled and said, 'Tell Wren that yes, he will finish his last year!'

"How did she know the name of my sister? How did she know that my sister and I talked about her friend's son finishing his last year of high school?

"I smiled and shook my head in disbelief at the precognitive intuitions this young women possessed.

"Three weeks later, Quirk called.

"'Bayou, how did you like Leslie?'

"Before I could answer, he kept on talking, 'She's a moon-child, second sight, and all that jazz. She can see and feel the dreads and joys of the future.

"'Quirk,' I said, 'I know you're calling for a reason, and it isn't to talk about Leslie.'

"'Well, that's why I called,' stuttered Quirk. 'In Charleston, South Carolina—actually, right off the Battery—we have a report of some ghost manifestations. Two things make this interesting: one, it appears in the daylight; and two, it's asking for you, by name. And get this, Bayou, it's specifically asking for *the son of Razor, father of Mist.* I have to go, but I'll e-mail all the particulars.' And with that he hung up.

"I felt a tsunami of epidemic fear. The Battery was where the people in Charleston joke that the Ashley and Cooper Rivers join to form the Atlantic Ocean. I think this spirit wants me one-on-one, *mano-a-mano.*

"I knew that I definitely wasn't up to a *mano-a-mano* fight. Just thinking of fighting a ghost was depressing and distressing at the same time. Especially in light of two very important things: it wasn't a fake, and it requested me by name.

"My brain seized on a slim ray of hope. The ghost must have asked for me because there is no one else left, I decided. The other rangers died in the battle with the Magi. The ghost doesn't really want me, I rationalized; it's just that there is no one else left to challenge.

"Trying to adjust to all this spiritual mumbo-jumbo was confusing. My spiritual condition was at a low and negative place.

"But I had learned some things about death that surprised me. First, there are two kinds of death. The primary death is systemic, meaning organ failure. The second death takes place at the cellular level.

"My quality training led me to try to comprehend the system of death, because quality is all about systems. Death is the omega system, unless, of course, you believe in the afterlife.

"Another interesting tidbit I learned about death was how police are able to reconstruct the face if there is a facial accident. The process involves taking the measurement of the forefinger parallel to the thumb gap. This gap is then put in place under the nose to the eyebrow bridge, or the under the chin to the nose gap to reconstruct the face.

"I heard the doorbell ring. I walked over to the door and saw a UPS driver with what appeared to be a large guitar case package.

"I pulled it out of the box, and sure enough, it was my Fender Esquire—the rebuilt version. The Institute had found original machine heads and everything looked original, but I knew that it was now a combo of Bob, Jon's, and my leftover magical music equipment.

"I pulled out a chord and plugged into my little Fender Bullet amp. It played well, especially on the front pickup, which was my favorite Fender sound. The action on the fret board was low and it was easy to bend the strings. I hit the fifth, seventh, and twelfth frets; the harmonics pinged and played well. Someone at the Institute had put a nine-gauge Fender Bullet set on, and I always loved the feel of new strings.

"Life was good! I reached out to see if I could *feel* any mojo. If it was there, it was entombed under the pick guard, waiting for the right time. I felt nothing; the magic was moot.

"I called Dad and told him the guitar had arrived.

"'Damn, son, why did you waste your time trying to get that thing to work? You know it only works when fighting, not practicing.'

"'Well, Dad, I thought it might be possible to do a performance rehearsal before I get to Charleston. Quirk called and said there is a ghost waiting for me down there.'

"I also told him that I had taken a hiatus from my company as a quality consultant, since Quirk said that money was no longer a problem. There was a severe shortage of investigators since the aftermath of the Magi. Of course after the lawyers, who knew what would be left? For now, though, they could pay me the same wages I had been making in my consulting role.

"'Dad, I figured I had better play the guitar in case I have to cover my ass when I get down there!

"'*Die-my-ass* reasoning is more like it. Bayou, you know that the guitar can only be accessed by the presence of evil. So why are you wasting time trying to activate it?

"'Haven't you learned anything, son? I tell you what. I'll see if I can clear my schedule to come down there with you.'

"I smiled. Here the man was retired and he still had to see if he can clear his schedule. He had been busy going to other Institutes, explaining what had happened at Woosley Heights. As far as he was concerned, it was a simple explanation. He said that only an idiot would try to complicate it. His one-minute explanation was this: The Magi was evil; we were good; we got lucky—end of story. Dad repeated the same thing in all of his dispositions.

"'Sure, Dad,' I said. 'I'll call Leslie to see if she can come along, too, but three weeks ago she mentioned that this was coming and that I would have to do this by myself.'

"'Quirk is coming here this afternoon,' Dad said. 'Why don't you come over and we'll talk.'

"I walked in and saw Dad talking to Quirk. 'Quirk says Leslie told him that this is a solo gig. That means I don't go, either. Leslie described a rite of passage for you, but don't worry. She said that you will come out healed, whatever that meant.'

"Dad continued. 'I called Leslie, introduced myself, and got down to business. She must have call-waiting, because she knew my name when she answered the phone.'

"Quirk and I shared a smile at that remark.

"Anyway, she said, 'Be Cool, Razor. It's already a done deal; he had to meet the ghost himself.' Then she laughed and told me not to worry, that everything was under control. Then she told me some shit that I had no clue how she found out about. She is a spooky one, isn't she? She was probably smoking that dope or something!

"Quirk and I both laughed.

"'What about the guitar, Dad?' I asked, trying not to sound as scared as I was. I didn't realize until now how desperately I wanted Leslie and Dad to be there, backing me up. Now I was being told that this was a minor evil. What the hell, literally, was a minor evil? How did you tell the difference between major and minor evils? Again, I felt like a dilettante in this psychic football game.

"Man, oh man. I could have used one of those old-time magic eight balls. All you had to do was shake it and roll it over and it would forecast the next move.

"All I knew was that I had to pick up the reconstituted Fender guitar. I still didn't know if the magic part of it had worked. Next I had to drive down to Charleston, which was about four and a half hours away, because I didn't want to put my guitar on an airplane and risk having it broken or stolen.

"Finally, I had to arrive in Charleston and go solo against a ghost who knew my name and address. Then, after my victorious battle with the ghost, life would somehow revert back to normal.

"Sounded pretty straightforward to me. What was there to worry about? After all, it was only a *minor* evil.

CHAPTER 16

✿

"I had been back in Waynesville after the fight—alive, coherent, and feeling juiced—when the phone rang several hours later. Quirk asked me, 'Hey, dude, what happened? Did you forget to call in? You've had Razor worried, and I was scared to death. Are you all right?'

"'Yeah, I'm fine,' I told Quirk. I explained the whole Charleston deal and said I would be better about calling in the future. I told him how I fought an old evil ghost and saw the ghost of my dead mother. I told him I was feeling weird and more confused than ever. I signed off, ready to catch some much needed rest.

"My head had barely hit the pillow when the phone rang again. This time it was Dad.

"'Well, son, how's it going? Tough day?'

"He sounded a little worried, but then he switched right back into his normal mode. He surprised me, though; instead of asking if I had broken anything in the encounter, he asked about the guitar.

"'How did the guitar work out? I wasn't sure that it would function again after that Woosley Heights episode.'

"I told Dad that it worked fine in the sudden-death playoff I had experienced, and that it now generated new super-powered five-star omniscience. I told him that it worked well, but that it had ultimately waited until the last minute to save the day.

"Dad laughed and said, 'No, son, that's normal. I think it's God's way of teasing the devil.'

"'I can say that I didn't appreciate it either, but when it does kick, it gets the job done. At least you don't have to play with catgut strings the way I had to. You boys have it made with the strings they make these days!'

"I knew that he was pulling my leg. It's the musician's version of *when I was your age I walked to school in 3 feet of snow for 5 miles, both ways uphill.*

"'Maybe,' he continued, 'it's some kind of mystic fate or something. It needs a bona fide challenge to make it jump up and shout.

"'Personally I wouldn't do it, but sometimes I think it would be nice to implant a piece of that neck up my ass just as a fail-safe.'

"I laughed. Dad is Dad. He's a real down-to earth pragmatist. He doesn't lose sleep if he can't figure something out. He figures, what the hell, why waste sleep on something that has no immediate answer? If the ghost of our most recent encounter had taken the power of the guitar away, then that was that. Don't lose sleep on what you cannot control.

"I finished restringing the guitar, and stretched out the new strings by playing one of my old favorites, *Standing On Shaky Ground*. I love those funk and blues songs. I started throwing out words, seeing if something fit. I threw out all the death words I knew: cold bodies, pallbearers, graveyard, coffins, funeral policies, and tombstone. It sounded kind of funny, singing the words *standing on* and then throwing in one of the death words. It sounded like the death blues were in business.

"Maybe I could start my own genre.

"The guitar played like a dream. There is nothing better than smooth frets on that weird oak fret board, a maple body, and low action to make me happy. The different character in the guitars I have played always intrigued me.

"This guitar was no exception. It had the Fender feel and taste. The messianic music it had played in Charleston had kept my music-playing butt out of the dark side of the graveyard. It would have made old Leo Fender proud of his baby.

"I looked down at my savior—my big wood pacifier. It was my security blanket and my savior in the ghost battles that I could not afford to lose.

"Surviving those ghostly encounters had been pure luck so far. The crash course was one hell of a ghost-fighter basic training. I knew it, and didn't even try to lie to myself about it.

"I was starting to come into my own with the guitar. When the battle-passion activated between the guitar and me, we merged into one for the main event.

"I have always been generous with my choices of music. The guitar didn't seem to care. I wondered if it needed a host to free its awesome thunder. It was a Taoist, eastern kind of thought. I followed the tangential thought: maybe all guitars react the same way.

"Would it make a difference what surroundings the wood was grown in? For example, if a person who had experienced events like broken promises, stolen money, and death had grown the wood, would it impact the playing?

"According to Quirk's research, the guitar neck had been taken from an old crucifix that had belonged to a saint.

"During the Charleston battle, right before the grand finale, I found myself pushing feral screams and distortions through the Fender guitar combination of pick, string, and volume.

"I looked down at the guitar again, the story continuing to unfold as I strummed the strings. After a while I was tired of playing, which was unusual for me. I felt an exhaustion of the spirit. It was time to cozy up next to my axe and take a much-needed rest.

"I woke up and looked at my clock; it said 666. I only smiled; I had seen that in enough movies that it didn't affect me. I looked at the guitar and saw that there was no glow. It was interesting how I slept with it beside me on the bed these days.

"My mind flashed to the email I had read before hitting the hay. I remembered something about Leslie calling me and telling me to look at my email. It said that Leslie, Dad, Quirk, and I needed to come to Woosley Heights tonight. The email also said that Razor and Leslie would die. Quirk and I were not mentioned.

"I called Dad, keeping an eye on the clock. It still read 666. I figured it must be around 7 A.M., or close to it.

"'Hi,' Razor answered.

"'Dad!' I blurted out. 'Have you heard the word?'

"'Yeah,' he said, 'it's no big deal; we all go when we go. I have everything prepared for you and your sister.' He sounded serious. 'I found out yesterday and called my lawyer; everything's arranged.'

'Son,' he continued, 'I have no insurance, just an accidental death policy through the Institute. Quirk has already called Leslie to make sure she was covered. Sounds like tonight is going to be a hell of a fight. I am sure as hell not going to roll over and play dead!' He didn't sound scared; he never had, since I could remember.

"He continued, 'I called all the grandkids and told them I loved them and that I was just was checking up on them. No use to mention tonight; there is nothing they can do, if this is the real deal.'

"Sounded like Dad; 'Don't worry anyone, just deal with it yourself.'

"Dad had always been prepared for emergencies. He had a natural contingency approach mindset.

"'We're supposed to meet up there at midnight,' he said. 'Why don't you and your sister come up and have supper around six? That will give us time to enjoy each other's company before we head off to fight this thing. Around eight we'll start getting ready.'

"'Sure, Dad,' I said. 'See you at six.'

"I sat there for awhile in a state of shock. The phone did not ring. I started to call Leslie, but changed my mind. I just sat and processed for a while.

"It's interesting. I wondered if everyone would want to know when they were going to die—if they somehow had the opportunity to know beforehand, that is. I know *I* would, but I couldn't speak for the rest of the population.

"If I did smoke, I would have lit up then. Hell, I would have settled for a quick toke of weak, homegrown pot, not that strong killer stuff that makes you stupid. I am a control freak and I have to feel in control of myself at all times.

"Dad was probably happy. He liked order and control, and here he was getting ready for his death. I was certain that Dad wouldn't be late for his appointment with death.

"If he did die, he would be the last of my elders. All my grandparents and my mother were gone. It was Dad who was caught at death's door.

"The exegesis of living and dying was going to happen tonight. I was resigned to it and felt weird about being so pragmatic. I was about to experience a cosmological showdown that would rupture my family life—and I was feeling no guilt or remorse. Was I mentally impaired, or just caught up in the aftermath of the experiences?

"My concerns unconsciously propelled me toward the phone. I called Quirk.

"He answered immediately and said, 'Bayou, I have intercepted all resources and intervened with everyone's plans. Everyone I can pull will be assisting, in every possible precaution tonight.'

"He sounded stubborn, as usual.

"'I hate this,' he said, 'and am prospecting all options!'

"'Quirk,' I said, my mental stamina is just not working for me. Do you have any explanations?'

"Quirk sighed. 'It sounds like we have to pay a price tonight for the business that we are in. I concur; my stamina is weak, too, but we can't just give in. I don't fraternize with others' realities, but this is a first. All of the agencies had a visit from Leslie, and have sent good-byes and best wishes to Razor. It blows my mind. I think we all believe that she is the real thing and that this is going to go down. I know that Leslie believes it to be so and has told her parents. She is spending a quiet day with them and expects this to be her last day on the planet.'

"'So,' I jumped in, 'the penalty for tonight is death.'

"'Yeah,' he said, and hung up.

CHAPTER 17

❀

"I picked up the guitar and left for Dad's place at 5:00 P.M.

"He was in good spirits, and we had a great supper. Wren cried, but kept a tough outlook. We discussed future options on the property and normal death dominoes.

"Being his typical self, Dad informed us that if there was a body left, we were to cremate it and have a service that lasted no longer than fifteen minutes—or his ghost would come back for us.

"The phone had been ringing the whole time we ate, and he finally just let the answering machine pick up. I mentioned it to Dad; he said it was people wanting his fishing gear and laughed. He said, 'If I'm dead, who cares, anyway?'

"Wren left and we cleaned up. At 11:00 we drove to Woosley Heights.

"We saw Quirk's car parked in front of the house, and watched as a flashlight came around the side of the house. It was Quirk and Leslie. Leslie had the Bloodstone with her, and had a serious look on her face.

"'Hey guys,' Dad said. 'We have about 40 minutes left.'

"Then he smiled that classic smile of his.

"Quirk handed each of us a headset and informed us that they were loaded with new batteries.

"It was then that reality hit us. I had been hoping for some sort of divine intervention, but it wasn't happening.

"I had my guitar strapped on; Leslie held the Bloodstone above her head. Dad positioned himself between us, somehow feeding off the nexus. Quirk talked to all of us through the headsets.

"I waited while my watch crept towards midnight. Finally I looked down right at the moment of the witching hour. I felt the air pressure change immediately.

"Four portals opened around the remnants of the house. The shadows of evil filled my nostrils.

"Quirk snapped out orders. 'Bayou, Leslie, strike the portal at one o'clock.'

"We both directed our energies into the portal. My D note and bottom four strings, augmented by the pure strength of Leslie's Bloodstone, gave birth to an incredible power surge.

"The portal lit up and imploded.

"'Quick! Quirk called out. 'Three o'clock!' We focused our energy into that portal and again met with success. A spectacular aurora borealis appeared, lighting up the southern night. The portal was pouring out power lines that colored and powered a gigantic 'Slinky' effect in Earth's magnetic field lines.

"'Nine o'clock!' Quirk yelled, and again we focused our energy. This time the energy beam seemed to split into the nearby foliage. I felt a stab of pain as a shaft of power slammed into me. This beam, or wave, passed energy to electrons, accelerating them along the magnetic field lines around Earth. When the electrons hit the atoms in the atmosphere, the atoms become excited and produced the colors of the aurora. We were putting on a hell of a light show for the planet. The portal imploded.

"'Six o'clock!' Quirk yelled. As I looked up, the last portal opened and a beam of light hit me point blank in the chest with the impact of a big rig truck running straight into me.

"Pain erupted again as I hit the ground.

"*There's no time for panic!* I thought. My mind screamed for action, but my body was too stunned to move. I felt the guitar being torn from my body.

"Dad pulled the guitar from me and started to move toward the portal. My primitive mind was screaming; if we couldn't close it, what chance did he have?

"I watched in disbelief as Dad grinned and began pouring the energy into the guitar. Something seemed to be coalescing inside the portal. He aimed the energy and played even harder than before. His guitar was in the process called reconnection; it was sending waves rippling through the magnetic field around the portal, like wiggling a Slinky.

"He yelled, 'Leslie, throw me the Bloodstone!' Leslie, in shock, threw it to him. He caught it with one hand and palmed it in his right pick hand.

"He looked back, as if in slow motion, and smiled. I knew at that moment that his consciousness was the price we'd have to pay to close the portal.

"Dad looked straight into the portal and started advancing, while playing the fastest heavenly licks I had ever heard. The guitar beam electrons were accelerating, showing sufficient energy from the Bloodstone to power a counter-aurora.

"Smoke was coming off his right hand and the top of his head. The Bloodstone must be doing something, as red lightning began pouring from the head into the portal. It looked like spontaneous combustion was erupting from Dad's right fist. He was playing faster and faster, while moving closer to the malediction inside the portal. A stream of charged particles from the guitar, transmitting energy to the portal, was unraveling the complex processes behind the larger-scale particle portal accelerations.

"Dad didn't care; he was working at a primal level. The portal wavered; jets of material were ejected from the black holes in the center of the portals.

"I saw Dad closing in for the kill.

"'No! This can't be happening! God, no!' I screamed as I tried to get up.

"In a panicky effort to quell the unwanted disaster coming, I tried to run to Dad. I felt another electric bolt run through me, knocking Leslie, Quirk, and me to the ground. I looked up and saw that Dad was still playing—in a haze of energy. Smoke was coming off of him everywhere. He was a haze of red lightning and a red glow.

"Whatever effigy that was trying to escape had not planned on meeting up with Razor Savage. I saw Dad take a couple of steps backward, but he still kept playing the guitar, leaning into the portal, putting all of his energy into closing it.

"It wasn't civilized or sophisticated, but Dad started moving closer to the violation. Bright red smoke was pouring from the guitar. I could tell the sound energy was violating the effigy trying to come out of the portal.

"Dad's features were lit up in the glow of the guitar. He reached the portal and pivoted the guitar straight into the effigy. Leslie screamed and broke free.

"She reached Dad and grabbed his right hand. She poured her energy into Dad, combining their powers.

"Her body leaned on Dad's, pushing them both toward the portal. I had always thought that it was the Bloodstone feeding Leslie, but I was wrong. It was more than just the Bloodstone. Leslie had powers of her own, and I realized then that she could kick ass even without the Bloodstone. It was her brainpower. I understood then that she was controlling the ghost mass with her own natural powers. She was using the Bloodstone to liberate the matter. Leslie understood that matter is energy waiting to happen; she was using the Bloodstone to square the energy inside herself. The Bloodstone just made her mega psychic in all dimensions.

"I could feel the heat coming off them. Through the waves of heat I saw that their psychic energy was scorching the portal. The fourth portal was now on fire.

"I screamed, still unable to move. From the corner of my eyes I saw Quirk, also frozen in place, screaming.

"Leslie and Razor had an affinity beyond anything I had ever seen. It was one of those moments that are memorable until the day you die.

"'Dad!' I screamed, thinking only *What are you doing to yourself?*

"Dad's hair was on fire. His clothes and Leslie's clothes were on fire, yet he and Leslie were somehow connected and continued to focus the energy of the guitar and the Bloodstone through both remaining portals.

"In a final characteristic gesture, Dad threw himself into the portal. Leslie joined him, which foredoomed both of them. I went into a panic as the portal exploded. In an instant I was knocked down, then blasted into another direction by the fourth portal closing.

"I knew I was looking at yet another change of boxers if I survived this. Oh God, I hurt all over!

"Smoke permeated and surrounded the house, inside and out. Visibility was about zero percent.

"'Quirk!' I screamed, realizing that I had lost my hearing. All I heard was the pounding in my head and a dull sense of nothingness. I tried to dance my head up into a seeing position.

"'Dad!' I yelled. 'Dad...Dad...Dad...Dad...' I kept yelling, wailing into the maelstrom, to no avail.

"I crawled toward the spot where I thought I had last seen him.

"Then I felt something weird at my side. I looked down and saw my cell phone lit up with an incoming message. Hell, I didn't remember bringing the damn thing with me! I picked it up and listened and didn't hear anything. That confirmed that my hearing was gone. I couldn't hear a damn thing.

"I felt like a cucumber at the pickle factory.

"I put the phone back on my belt and didn't think about it further.

"'Dad!' I yelled again, and noticed something out of my peripheral vision. It was Quirk, and he was crawling toward the same destination. There was no light except this sparkling, diminishing fireworks show coming from where the portals used to be.

"Everything went quiet. I met Quirk at what used to be the third portal. We found the two burnt, charred bodies, grotesquely entwined in some macabre dance The smell of smoldering, incinerated flesh hung in the air like the stench from a paper mill on a calm day.

"I lost it. I started blubbering like a kid with a broken toy on Christmas Day. My head was in a tailspin—and I had had enough. I knew the charred bodies were Dad and Leslie. They had sacrificed themselves, closing the portal. Some mysterial ritual had succeeded with the combination of the guitar and the Bloodstone.

"I lay there for what seemed like forever. I was sick. I knew that Dad was finally gone. I didn't know whether to laugh or cry—that sick reaction to horror we get when a disaster overwhelms propriety. *He went out the way he lived*, I thought. *No bullshitting around; just get the job done.*

"If he were here, I could imagine exactly what he'd say.

"'Get your scrawny ass up and cover her body.' He wouldn't give a shit about his own, but Leslie's body needed to be covered.

"I took my jacket off and covered them both. They were locked in that twisted embrace of death—I guessed her body was the smaller one. They were so burnt up I couldn't tell.

"Then I thought I heard him say, 'Get up; call her parents and get these bodies out of here. There is no utility in crying over the dead. Figure out what's next and get to it, boy. It's all on you now, son.'

"Slowly, I leaned back against what was left of the wall and regathered my strength. I felt like a drunk. My brain was moving slow and my body was slower.

"I finally heard a noise, happy to know that the hearing loss wasn't permanent. It was Quirk yelling, right beside me.

"'What?' I yelled back.

"He yelled. 'Let's get these bodies back to the Institute!'

"I was frozen in place. My brain was saying something about moving evidence at a crime scene. What a joke!

"I damn near laughed. No detective investigating this place would ever be able to figure out what had happened. Not with any amount of forensic tricks, never, ever.

"So I held my breath and crawled away from the portal, anxious to get some fresh air into my seared and aching lungs.

CHAPTER 18

❀

"I accepted it. I labored with it and accepted their choices. The funeral was a success. I did the eulogy the same way I had done it for Mom. Wren, Mist, and all of the family and friends showed up. Dad would have been proud. Everyone smiled. He went out with style. No stroke, no heart attack, and no diabetes dismemberment. He had fought the good fight a fight to save the planet. And by God, he had won!

"He was a physic Purple Heart Winner. His death caught me off guard. *Are we ever prepared for a parent's death?* I asked myself for the millionth time.

"His lovers, friends, and fellow fishermen all showed up. It looked like half of Haywood County had known and respected, if not loved, my old man. He died at seventy-five years of age, while fighting an unknown enemy. The official story was that he had perished in a gas explosion.

"He had grabbed the guitar from me, thereby sacrificing himself in place of me to close the portal. It left an unsatisfying taste in my mouth. There was an emptiness in me that I didn't know if it could ever be completely filled.

"I chose not to belong to the victimization industry. I moved on. He had made his choice. Maybe it was pre-ordained. Maybe he and Leslie had reached enlightenment.

"I attended Leslie's funeral the day after Dad's.

"The climate there was sadder. She was younger, and an only child, which makes for a really sad funeral.

"The distinctions between her funeral and Dad's were not lost on me. There were a lot of college students at Leslie's funeral. Three of them gave a small narrative of her contribution to their lives and how she died too early. The papers had the same story for Leslie as they did for Dad. She died in a gas explosion.

Nobody made the connection or saw the coincidence. The Institute funded both funerals. The Institute turned out in full force.

"The other distinction was the obvious lack of celebration. With Dad, the attendees had a *he-lived-a-lot-longer-than-I-thought-he-would* type of smile. With Leslie's, she just hadn't lived long enough.

"I somehow had that eerie *X-Files* feeling that my time was just around the bend. What was left of the guitar was a skeleton. The Bloodstone had fused itself into two new pickups. This feat must have happened during the epic deaths of Dad and Leslie.

"Quirk had the Institute work and remake the guitar. The pickups—infused with the Bloodstone—worked perfectly. I tried it out. It felt just like before.

"My depression, though, was a different story. It was late at night on June 26. My will was in place and everything was taken care of. I was going to try an experiment. My head had been through too much, and I couldn't take any more.

"The depression hadn't lifted. Quirk tried to make me feel better, saying that the closing of the portals bred my melancholy. We had shut down the evil ghost connection for good.

"I was too tired to teach, too tired to parent, too tired to be a hero. I had given it my best shot and was tired. The drinking hadn't helped; I just wanted to be alone, and I had figured out a way to do it.

"The phone rang. It was Quirk.

"'Bayou,' he said, 'we're getting mixed signals on 2012, but I think we're going to need your help.'

"'Sure,' I said. 'I'll see you around 9 A.M.'

"Everything was ready. My plan was simple. I just wanted to rest for a while. I had read about Merlin putting King Arthur into a trance.

"I grabbed the guitar. I could feel its power, now enhanced with the Bloodstone pickups.

"I thought about all the people I had inspired and all the good times. I wanted to experience that feeling again. I wanted Dad and Mom back. I wanted Mist to be my little daughter again, not grown up the way she was.

"'Damn, Bayou, you are a mess!' I said. Tears spilled onto the E and A strings and rolled down to the bottom B and E. The funk wouldn't go away. All my anger was turned inward. In the end, I hadn't been good enough. Not good enough to help shit! I couldn't help Mom, Dad, Leslie, Jon, Bob, or Mist. I felt like a failure. I managed a pissed-off kind of smile. As Anthony Robbins would have said, *I am depressing.* It is a verb, not a noun. I choked on a sardonic laugh.

"I thought of my life and began playing the guitar. I felt myself sinking into the Bloodstone pickups. I knew it had the power to give me what I wanted.

"I wanted to be like Rip Van Winkle in the Washington Irving story. I wanted to rest twenty years and resurface.

"I had made provisions for Mist; I had told my girlfriend she was my undying love, but neither of them would understand. I hoped they would forgive me for taking a twenty-year sabbatical. I knew it was selfish, but I was cashed. I was a hollow shell that seriously needed replenishing.

"I inhaled the heavy smell of wildflower blossoms that were blooming next to the house. I thought I could hear the trees singing in the wind, singing and playing for the joy of it, the way I wanted to be.

"The pickups started to glow and I hit a low, breathy pitch on the E string. I thought of sleeping beneath an old shade tree, my spirit and energy replenished. Big, wet depressed tears rolled down my cheeks as I saw a reddish glow starting to surround my soul.

"Sweet surrender."

CHAPTER 19

✿

Steve was writhing, and felt a voice that wasn't Bayou's coming to him. He wasn't sure whose it was, but it was completing Bayou's circle for Steve and everyone watching the videos at the Institute.

Quirk found the body the afternoon of the next day. After Bayou had missed his appointment, Quirk became worried and investigated. Some sixth sense told him what he would find. He moved the body to the Institute by positioning and repositioning the guitar, before the body could disparate. This was a feat that was never duplicated. Only Quirk had been able to accomplish it. He instantly put his best scientists on it. Bayou's girlfriend and Mist couldn't believe he would ever do this. They hadn't realized how serious his depression had been. He had taken one too many psychic and physical punches and had taken a sad way out.

Two years later, Quirk disappeared. No note, no trace of him could be found. Interesting, because Mist and Bayou's girlfriend disappeared at the same time. Detectives tried to make the connection, but no one could give any feedback. The story made the news, and more than a few tried to make the disappearance a psychic event. The Institute knew for sure that there had been no psychic events since Razor's death.

Then 2012 hit and Bayou and Quirk were delegated to the back burners.

Suddenly, alarms sounded as the videos faded for the last time. All hell broke loose in a time sliver. Everyone panicked and regained freedom of motion at the same time. It sounded like a hysterical crowd in a stadium.

Oswalt yelled, "Where is that alarm coming from?"

"It's Steve!" someone yelled. "He's coming out of his memory scan." The side of Steve's head had split open and blood was everywhere. He opened his eyes and was confused. His last memory was a red glow and a peaceful feeling. Everyone was looking at him, worried—and where was his guitar? Had he slept longer than twenty years? He was Bayou reawakened. Wasn't he?

"Steve, Steve!" People were yelling a name and surrounding him, injecting him with liquids. Someone was putting an oxygen inserter in his mouth. The oxygen helped clear away some of the cloud of confusion. There was a woman who looked strangely familiar; she looked sad and very concerned.

He wondered if she was Mist. He tried to speak, even to whisper, but his throat forgot how to work. Oswalt looked worried.

"What time is it?" Oswalt asked, trying to restore order.

The alarms abated as someone told him it was 6 A.M. He knew sunrise was in ten minutes.

"How's Steve?" he asked.

Jade responded. "He's alive, but confused; he's disconcerted from the scan. I think it's normal," she said, never taking her eyes off Steve. It was clear that Steve was trying to recognize her.

They cleared the blood off of him. He had a serious bite on his cheek. He had been wearing a mouthpiece, which probably protected him from worse injury. A clamoring sound made everyone turn around.

The coffin was floating in midair; all of the monitoring equipment had fallen off to the side. It was accompanied by an orgasmic release of energy. The velocity suddenly subsided, and Oswalt felt like his brain had been diced.

The technicians regained composure and were trying to gently subdue Steve. He clamped his hand on one of them and tried pulling himself up.

It was all coming back to him now. He was Steve Johnson, not Bayou Savage. He understood. *He understood*!

Steve had trouble organizing his thoughts, but he knew that the coffin floating was not normal.

He had to do something. He yelled at the technician next to him. "Release me! Hurry up, dammit!" Did he just say dammit, or was it the residual effect of being Bayou?

Jade helped Steve get the straps off. Oswalt was standing with the other scientists, as close to the coffin as they could. Brown ran out of the room, screaming. Everyone froze and just stared at the floating coffin.

It floated there, defying gravity. Inside the coffin, the guitar glowed red and suddenly blasted the top of the coffin into shredded projectiles. The floating, now topless shredded coffin, amplified the visual mystery, shearing their already shattered brains. It was then that the guitar floated up and began a slow rotation.

Steve's subconscious mind thought that this couldn't' be happening; nothing could foster a force that could defy or decrease two hundred years of quantum stasis. Yet the guitar remained floating, resting on nothing.

The burnt yellow fringes and blood red-pickups were pulsating with power. Time seemed eternally slow for all of those watching. Steve finally shook loose and ran over. He struggled to remember the name of the lovely woman who had helped him out of the restraints.

The DNA memory scan shouldn't have been doing this. He had a wild thought: this event reeked implicitly of the Halloween factor.

An implosion suddenly occurred where the red tendril had been tethered to the wall. A portal opened up in its place. Hanging there, devoid of any incumbencies, were two figures. Their silhouettes were soft and powdery in the light.

Then, in a conspicuously hurried manner, Razor Savage walked into the room, followed by Leslie. He examined the room with a glance and saw the occupants looking at him. His stern look said that he didn't care if he had violated the sanctity of the Institute's most private room.

The red light highlighted them, making the appearance even more dramatic. A hissing sound was coming from somewhere in the background.

Steve just stood there, thinking *This can't be.*

"Dad," he whispered, and then he shook his head again, trying to remember who he really was.

"Dammit, Leslie, is that the guitar? I can't focus my eyes yet. I feel it, but…" he yelled, as he tried to grab the guitar.

Everyone froze, gawking at the two memories coming to life in front of them. It was the unsubstantial images from the video screen becoming "real life," not a virtual reality. They both looked incredible. Steve was the first to notice that they were dressed the same way they were when they had…"died."

How could they be alive?

Steve moved forward, but was blocked by the reddish cocoon force field surrounding the coffin.

Leslie walked right through it, discharging the force field like a ghostly waif. She grabbed the well-burnished guitar and slung it at Razor. She looked, all in all, like the co-redemptirix that she was.

Razor grabbed the guitar in midair and threw the burnt axe around his body. There was no awkwardness, no fumble, and no folly. His image affixed to them as they watched in wonder and worry. It was the same maneuver they had watched him display in the scans.

Jade stared in amazement. My God—it really was Razor, and he was trying to rescue Bayou. She knew it intuitively. The thought provoked her subconscious mind, something about that had been imprinted at the first voice of the video. *What was it?* she wondered, and then she knew, as she looked at him.

It exploded into her conscious detailed mind. The second input recoded on the videos had not been Bayou—it had been Razor Savage all along, letting them access Bayou's memory.

That had been the second tendril coming out of the wall. When they began the experiment, it hadn't been there. It only surfaced when the video started to download. She remembered the opening words...

"Why are you trying to access his memory?" the voice had asked.

Razor had given them access to Bayou's memory. Why?

He walked in with no grandiose need for recognition. Yet where had he and Leslie been for the past two hundred years?

There was no time for thought as Razor strummed down on the guitar. The guitar glowed bright white and red streaks and triangulated on the body of Bayou Savage, resting in the coffin.

Everyone but Jade, Steve, and Oswalt moved back. They watched the guitar, transfixed. The pressure in the room increased tenfold. The old, burnt guitar flared to supernova energy. Steve stared in total disbelief, smelling an energy aroma in the air.

Jade was enthralled. Razor was more incredible than the videos had recorded. His activity released a natural resurfacing of rage and anger as he directed the guitar's energies toward the coffin.

Leslie was robust and beautiful as she reached out to touch the guitar. She radiated action, red energy flowing from her fingertips. They looked like legends, larger than life, come back to life. They acted in concert with an Everest of sound and light forming behind them. The room was oscillating, and Steve felt like he was experiencing a psychic earthquake.

Razor and Leslie were concentrating their energies into the coffin. The room oscillated around them, and they could all feel the vibrations intensifying. Extraordinary colors were reflecting off the coffin.

Jade held her breath. Her mind was detached as she saw the coffin taking great lurches, bursting with the inflow of the red energy flares. Winds were being generated and were gusting at hurricane strength from their affront on the coffin.

Steve grabbed the closest rail and hauled himself onto it for balance. He was still weak, but wouldn't miss this show for anything. The universe was experiencing energy it not felt in over two hundred years. The walls were vibrating, prey to the random energy ricochets. There was an incredible explosion, and he heard the crash of equipment and the sound of a door slamming somewhere in the building. For a fraction of a moment, he thought he would die.

Oswalt felt the blast and brought his arm up to protect his face and head. The explosion was a race in agonizing slow motion. It took forever, as if mired in molasses.

Some force was released from the coffin and shot straight through the ceiling. The air was instantly thick with falling debris and a deflating pressure. Oswalt, in a stupor, wondered neurotically if the ventilation fans were still working.

His adrenalizing thoughts of survival overrode any Institute imperative in his consciousness. His body, though, evoked the Fifth and just sat there, frozen in paralysis.

The coffin started slowly moving back toward the floor. Razor and Leslie hesitated as they followed it down with their eyes. The red force field was gone. Razor swatted aside some falling debris.

CHAPTER 20

All around, it was quiet. They all moved to look in the coffin.

Bayou rolled his head to the right. His corporal body was now taking on solid dimensions. He looked peaceful, but overheated. Three other bodies materialized beside the coffin. They looked vaguely familiar, and they were wearing antique clothing.

Leslie yelled, "Everyone freeze!"

All eyes stayed on the coffin, watching the physical changes to Bayou's body.

Taking on solid dimensions, his body started to breath. They watched as he slowly became solid, but nonmoving.

Steve was mesmerized. Would Bayou be all right? Bayou had blasted a permanent hole in his soul. He had flattened his emotions and dumbed his logical mind. For the past few hours, Bayou Savage had conditioned him, and he knew he would never forget it.

They had been through so much together; he *had* to be all right! For Mist's sake—if nothing else—and then he realized that he still shared Bayou's paternalistic memories. He had retrieved that one unconsciously.

Razor reached down, and for the first time in two hundred years, touched the face of Bayou Savage. Leslie stood over the body that they now had to wake up.

Razor spoke. "Hi, Mist, Quirk. It took you damn long enough to get here!"

Leslie laughed. Standing next to them, Razor took command of the space.

Oswalt had a smile on his face—he wasn't quite sure why—but this was history, and he was witnessing it. He didn't even remember his position, or anything else; only the event mattered.

The presence of Razor was powerful, immediate, and crowded the room. Steve thought, unconsciously, "Dad, you came back for me." Then he realized the duality of the thought.

"Bayou," Razor spoke his name softly, a paternalistic concern showing on his face. No one said a word.

If Razor Savage wanted to talk to his son, no one in the room was going to stop him. Steve felt like saying, "Dad, I'm here!" Somehow he restrained himself, barely remembering who he was. He still felt the Bayou connection; still felt that he was Bayou.

Razor put his hand behind Bayou's head and lifted it. He needed no justification for what he was doing. With great tenderness, great energy, he cradled Bayou's upper body.

Steve couldn't believe what he was seeing. The body was untouchable. He had personally been trying to touch that body during his entire tenure at the Institute. It was *his* body—no, it was *Bayou's* body. He tried to shake the cobwebs out of his brain. The merger was still in effect.

"Damn, I wish we had some of Quirk's elixir!" Razor snapped.

"Bayou, wake up! Come on, son, snap out it. You've been loafing for too damn long—we have work to do."

Jade couldn't believe Razor's choice of words. Not sympathy, but caring. He acted the way he had in the videos. He seemed to show no aftereffects of stress or adrenaline.

"Come on, Bayou! Wake up. Talk to me, son!" He gently rotated Bayou's lifeless head. It had no effect on Bayou.

Leslie jumped in with the guitar, also showing no signs of fatigue. "Let me try," she said gently, so as not to diminish Razor's effort.

Steve said, "Jade, put the oxygen inserter on him." Jade moved forward to stand next to Leslie and opened Bayou's mouth. She was afraid that she would stick the inserter in too far.

They all looked at him, desperate for some kind of movement. All was still for a moment, and then he breathed. It was as if time was occurring in baby steps, event by event.

Jade had slid the inserter tube completely in. She bumped the guitar by mistake, and was glad there was no crack of energy.

Razor still had his hand supporting Bayou's back and head.

Leslie diverted her attention to the guitar's pickups. She closed her eyes and focused her mental probe to the energy source of the Bloodstone. Red power cords elevated and surrounded her head. The cords paused for a second, and then shot out into Bayou's forehead.

Her mouth hung open, agape for a moment, as she focused her power. She said, "Razor, I'm going to try to open the doorway to his mind."

She focused, and Bayou's body jumped in response. The effect was almost like a comical act of sadistic terrorism.

Oswalt spoke in disbelief. "Are you sure you're not killing him?"

"No," she responded, as sweat started to form on her brow. "I'm trying to minimize the dimensional effect on him and steer his conscious mind to a waking state."

She spoke softly. "It's time to wake up, Bayou. You have rested, and now it's time. The time you dreamed of is here. It is safe. It is safe. It is safe. She kept repeating it as the power bonds pulsated. "It is time for Rip Van Winkle to wake up; it is time." Her voice slowly faded.

Tears trickled slowly down Bayou's cheeks.

Leslie whispered to Razor, her eyes never leaving Bayou's face. "He's bubbling back to consciousness, Razor. I can feel him. The connection is working."

Mist struggled to her feet, wiping away her own tears. She called out, her voice shaking. "Dad, I'm here. I need you. Please come on back."

The reddish glow softened as Leslie released her power. She had erected a bridge for Bayou to cross; it was up to him to cross it—or not.

Bayou struggled. He rolled his head to the sound of the voices that were surrounding him.

His first whispered words were, "Damn, Dad, I relived it all. But, but, you, you're dead!" He paused, and then slowly added, "How did you get here? Mist, is that really you? Quirk, Leslie?"

Then, with great effort, he opened his blue eyes. Oswalt was closest and couldn't believe how blue Bayou's eyes were. They were crystal blue; Razor's were a crystal gray.

Bayou turned and pulled Razor to him. He then hugged his dad for the first time in over two hundred years.

Leslie, Mist, Bayou's girlfriend, and Quirk all joined in with the hug. There were smiles around the room. The Hangar 19 mystery had been solved. As they said in the ancient book *Dune*, the sleeper had awoken.

Steve realized that he had been holding his breath, and he let it go. He turned and looked for Jade. He had sensed her caring presence throughout the experiment. She had been a lifeline—a reason to return, to struggle through the pain and regain his identity. Jade turned to Steve and held him close. She never wanted to let go, never again wanted to fear that she had lost Steve.

Epilogue: Six months later.

❀

The Hangar had disappeared and Steve missed it. He and Jade had many discussions as the Hangar was dismantled and reassembled for some other project. He didn't care; he had decompressed, decompartmentalized, de-everythinged. He was on top of the world, for a lot of different reasons. The Savages—Razor, Bayou and Mist—along with Leslie, Bayou's girlfriend, and Quirk were all off getting acquainted with this time period. Steve had learned that Razor had already raised enough hell to get in trouble with the law. He laughed out loud at the thought of how Razor was Razor, and that was that!

Jade and Steve had made the overt-love-commitment, and his lifelong loneliness was finally coming to an end. He loved the way she looked at him; he could feel her love and trust. She told him she felt like writing a book, and it would be a good project for both of them.

An added bonus was Jade's appreciation of his new hobby—playing that ancient musical instrument, the guitar.

Steve was now an accomplished guitar player, a pleasant byproduct of the experiment. He could play and go into an intuitive trance…Of course all the songs he knew were over two hundred years old, but what the hell! Those old songs sounded better anyway.

Steve reached down and carefully picked up his ancient guitar, a gift from the Savages. It was time to play some rock and roll. He found the power cord and plugged into the little amp they had made. Then, with a big grin, he turned the distortion to full volume.

He smiled as he stroked the opening lick to "Purple Haze." *I hope I don't break the pick this time.*

0-595-29599-1